FRIENDS, LOVERS, OR NOTHING

To Abby,

Enjoy the read and thanks for everything.

L. Maxwell

Dedication

I dedicate this work to my loving wife, Tiffany. Thank you for your kindness and sharing your light into my world. You have helped me become the person I am today, and I am forever grateful.

To Tamisha, you are a godsend. I am glad to still call you my friend.

To God and My Family, for bringing me up.

To the many others who tolerate my humor at work, school, and life.

To my friends Kevin, Curtis, Kurt, Mark, Julius, and Sean for being the jerks and brothers from another mother that you are to me.

And to the reader who decided to support this book, I am sincerely grateful. I hope you enjoy reading this as much as I enjoyed writing it.

Introduction

This book is about that moment in life that defines the rest of your life. You will forever look back at this moment and recall how it molded you into the person you are today. Falling in love is easy. But picking yourself back up after falling out of love is what develops us the most. It's better to have loved and lost, then to never loved at all. But I would challenge Shakespeare that love for yourself is the greatest.

It's not your average love story, but it could be if you think about it long enough. Best friends, lovers, enemies, random encounters, and self-reflection all told from Aaron's perspective. I hope you get a few laughs and most importantly, I hope you enjoy reminiscing.

Chapter One

Computer Blues

Who knew today was going to end up this way? I woke up in my usual fashion, a half hour later than when my alarm rang, wearing the same work clothes I prepped the night before. I was tired and I needed to exhaust every minute of sleep I could afford. My summer job has been asking me to put in extra hours lately. I was not one to complain, but my eighteen-year-old body was definitely feeling the toll. I race to my car and try to think of an excuse to tell my girlfriend for why I was running late for lunch--other than "I was sleep". But in my mind, I just keep thinking about how tired I have been lately.

My job wasn't labor intensive; it just required me to be on my feet for 12 hours at a time wielding a pneumatic drill. I had become quite the craftsman at my role in the assembly line--good enough to be told by my supervisor that I better not come back after I quit for college. Don't get me wrong, I enjoy working alongside passionate hard-working adults, but even they saw my potential. They kept encouraging me to study hard and shoot for the stars. It was as if they were correcting missteps in their life by giving me their unsolicited advice. I just shrugged it off as modestly as I could. I was not anyone special in my mind, but the look in my supervisor's eyes was that of a woman with broken dreams. She would always tell me how her sons were bouncing around life and it was difficult being a single parent. I had only known her for two months, but a part of me wanted to make her proud.

"Aaron, your dumbass better not come back here to work for me," Ms. Jones commanded.

"Why I got to be all that, Ms. Jones?" I reply trying to be considerate of her feelings.

"Because if you were smart, you'll come back here and I'll be working for you!" She said smiling. This was her way of complimenting me.

But, falser words have never been spoken. I have no intentions of coming back to work here after college. My goals consist of either becoming a doctor or a business owner. But if either of those fail, a published author at the age of thirty. I am sure my parents would want me to be a doctor.

As I was pulling my car into the parking garage of the mall, I got a text asking for my whereabouts. It was Helen. I figured she was not happy with my lack of punctuality. I replied that I will meet her in the food court. I made sure not to arrive empty handed, so I bought an iced mocha Frappuccino as an olive branch. She didn't seem amused by

2

me for the least bit when I did finally show; but she didn't seem too upset either. I could tell that she had been waiting there in spirit much longer than she had actually *been* there. Helen's demeanor suggested that she had been wrestling with this exact moment for some time. She wouldn't even look me in the eyes at first. Her hands cupped the drink I brought her—the drink was sweating from condensation, mirroring the look on my face.

"We need to talk," She whispered.

I could feel the pit in my stomach swell. I managed to lose my appetite while looming over the impending conversation.

"Let's go to your car." she insists.

As we are walking, I take notice of the many faces in the crowd. People are looking up at me as I glance at them. I am easily ignored and unnoticed. I was desperately hoping to see a familiar face, wishing someone would interrupt this solemn moment. Then I looked at Helen's face and realize how today was going to be unforgettable. We get to my car and I pretend to adjust various mirrors and push the buttons on the radio--anything to prolong the start of our conversation. But in my mind, I've already accepted what's to come. Helen's posture was distant, her voice softened, her hands cold.

I could tell she wanted to break up with me. I would be lying if I said this came as a surprise. Our conversations had become ever more shortened since graduation; texts seemed to be the only mode of communication. I felt this moment coming when I started receiving sporadic messages littered with apologies of conveniently dead batteries and the misplacement of phone chargers. I would just pretend it was the truth, because accepting reality was more difficult. The reality was this relationship may have been dead on arrival. Helen was clearly hiding her acknowledgment of the fact. (Somehow, I managed to be late to this conclusion as well. Just like I was late for lunch.)

"Is there someone else?" I asked knowing the answer was no.

"Of course not!" she told me convincingly.

"Then what is it?" I say as I begin to doubt myself, doubting my self-worth.

"I realize that we are not meant for one another. We have different goals, different beliefs, different needs…" she recites.

"My goal was to be with you for the rest of my life. I truly believed you loved me. And I needed to love you." I interjected, clearly disrupting her monologue.

The tears in her eyes were uncontrollable at this point. I was compelled to kiss them as they rolled down her face. She bit my lip and then pressed her forehead against my nose. Now my eyes begin to drown because I realize that this was not just about what *I* had envisioned for us. I never saw it from *her* perspective. Jade colored eyes cascading in a pool of heartache—reflecting the light tan hue of her skin. My teeth stammered to catch the words I wish to say. I apologize instinctively, as if that was what was needed to be said. This has to be my fault. How could I hurt someone this much?

For Helen, she was torn with the reality of our relationship. While I precariously managed her emotions trying to save up money by working long nights, she was previewing the next four years to come. I would be headed to a college many hours away; she was choosing to stay here in Memphis.

She asked me to promise her we would still be friends. In my mind, I wanted to say no. In my heart, I wanted to tell her I was saving for an engagement ring. I was wanting her to promise me we'd be together. How ironic that we ended up here on two opposite sides of different coins. I tell her, "I'll always be your friend." She left after kissing me again.

I drove away and parked my car in front of a jewelry store located near Best Buy. I stared at the double pane window of advertisements embellishing the marketing of love and happiness. I grimaced at the store clerk as she made a frown upon my work attire. Angrily in my head, I wondered why this dusty woman looked so judgmental. I looked down to avoid eye contact. Then I noticed that I managed to spill coffee on my shirt between the mall and now. I proceeded to walk into the Best Buy and make conversation with another human being, just to hear my crackled voice muffle through words caused by the congestion of crying. "Where is your Electronics Department?"

FRIENDS, LOVERS, OR NOTHING

The blue shirt employee looked at me like I was a slice of burnt toast. I started walking towards the monitors near the back of the store. Surrounded by fellow students and their parents, I could finally grasp the gravity of what just transpired. Everyone was here to get a deal on back to school specials; my problems were insignificant. I was just there to get away from having to look at my phone for a text that may never come.

Funny that I expected today to be like any other day. Get up, go to lunch, go to work, sleep, and repeat. I was living a frugal routine because I thought my life was figured out. I had saved up quite a bit for someone my age--hoping to sort between the 4 C's of carat, cut, clarity, and color. But now, I am staring at the blips of screensavers and ticket prices trying to decipher gigahertz, gigabytes, contrast ratios, and operating systems. I went from madly in love this morning to buying a laptop instead.

Chapter Two

Outside the Window

I place my new purchase in the trunk of my car. I do the customary three hundred-sixty degree look around to make sure no one is trying to jack my stuff. My sixth sense don't tingle, so it must be okay to leave it in there while I am at work. The drive to work takes about twenty-five minutes, which equates to 5 songs of trying to reset my emotions. The first song is a classic ballad, "Daniel Bedingfield's - If you're not the one".

"Oh no, I can't be listening to this right now." I change the track and catch the middle chorus of 'You are not alone'. "Not you, too, MJ. Just beat it."

I finally settle on listening to a talk radio station. The subject matter was around school funding and whether we should vote to increase taxes.

"We have Martin Williams on the line, local resident of Memphis, TN--and he opposes the tax bill. Tell us what made you against raising taxes, Martin?"

"Wassup man, I'm on the air? Well you see, when you look at the bigger picture, you got to realize that spending is growing at a higher rate than revenue is increasing. And plus, they got radio hosts like you on the air breathing up all the good oxygen, smelling like a box of AAA batteries. McDouble head…"

The call drops. Apparently it was a prank caller. He made a good point, even all the way up to the end. I couldn't help but break out into laughter as I realized how hilarious my city can be. If school funding cannot be taken seriously, maybe I should lighten up? I pull up into the right lane and wait in line to check in with the guard.

"How's it going Aaron? You know your shirt got a stain on it, right?" the guard jests.

"Yeah man I know. You know your hairline is crooked, right?" I rebutted.

We both laugh and I proceed to park in the back of the lot. Had I gotten here sooner, I would be able to park closer to the time clock. It really doesn't matter because the job is going to work me twelve hours anyways. It is summertime, people get hot, and we make air conditioners--do the math.

The bell rings which signifies we have five minutes to get our line ready to receive instructions. I leave my phone in the car and meander my way to meet up with Ms. Jones. She smiles and is happy to see me--she gives me the customary, borderline, sexual harassment wink. I forcefully smile and wait for my assignment.

I usually put on the air conditioner's side panels or I am the one screwing in the side panels. Today I found out I'll be doing both since a few people didn't show up for work today. Most people get upset when this happens. But today, the mundane, repetitive work was a godsend to keep my brain preoccupied. For the next 6 hours, all I hear are the muffled sounds of drills whirring, metal panels clanging, and the consistent hum of the coil factory in the distance. The bell ringing signifies that is it is now break time.

I go out to my car to eat lunch just to realize I forgot to bring a lunch. I'm starving, too. There was still some lukewarm coffee in my car. I grab my phone out the glove box to see 3 notifications. 2 messages, 1 call, 1 voicemail.

One message was from my mother informing me that I left my lunch in the fridge. The other message was from Helen. The call and voicemail were from Terri, Helen's friend. I listen to the voicemail first.

"Hey, Aaron... I heard what happened. I'm sorry. If you ever need to talk, let me know. I'm not trying to start any drama but I just know where Helen is coming from and sometimes people need closure. I feel like you are a great person and I personally don't know why things ended the way they did for you and Helen. Call me back."

Then I read Helen's text reluctantly.

"I hope you aren't mad. Thanks for understanding. Sorry."

FRIENDS, LOVERS, OR NOTHING

At this moment, my heart sank. I'm in a range of emotions. I'm curious about what Terri wants, angry at myself for forgetting my lunch, hungry as hell, sad to be single, and still madly in love with Helen. Reading her words made me feel as if today was just a figment of my imagination. The fact that she took the time to reach out to me made me feel as if she was going to change her mind, and we would be fine. I wanted to shake off the day and tell myself "You'll be fine." But this damn coffee stain on my shirt says otherwise. I remember now that the coffee spilled on me as I leaned over to kiss her. This mark reminded me that no matter how unscathed I appear, I was damaged. Clearly, there must be something wrong with me. I should've been more involved, more attentive, and showed more concern for whatever gaps were there to pry us apart. "How could I not see this coming?" I think to myself. But for some reason, deep down, I can't shake the belief that may be all for the best.

The only feeling left for me to feel now is numbness and sure enough it sets in hard. I don't even want to eat right now. There's fifty minutes left for my lunch break. I sit in my car and just wait desperately to hear the bell ring to call me back in to finish the shift. I have to stop beating myself up. I settle on the thought that there was nothing I could have said to sway her to change her mind. Yet, my fingers itch to text Helen as if she still loved me the way I love her. I checked her profile page on Facebook to see if she's posted anything. Nothing. It's such a strange feeling, I feel powerless.

Yesterday, I would not hesitate to write on all of her shares and comments. Now, I am afraid to even like her posts. Thankfully she hasn't posted anything. I quickly decide to deactivate my Facebook to keep myself from being tempted to see her on my timeline. It just hurts too much to deal with right now. I know it would be easier to just unfriend her, but then I would have been lying about us being able to maintain a friendship. Knowing Helen, she's probably also lurking on my page at the moment. Usually, I am posting witty stories about politics, cat videos, or rambling about whatever sports ball event is on TV. I could easily text her a message, but I believe that deactivating my account would send a clearer message. I have yet to decide on whatever message that may be. The bell whistles. I leave my car and throw the half empty Frappuccino across the parking lot. It lands on someone else's car and splashes on the outside of their window.

Chapter Three

Be Cool

It's been a few days now since I've spoken to Helen. The weekend was here and I'm the first one to wake up in the house. I walk into the bathroom and stare at my now paler face in the mirror. I haven't spent much time in the sun at all this summer. My hair has grown quite a bit and has been left unmanaged. I can see that my stomach protrudes to the side more and my chest is less flattering than it was this past spring. I stopped working out after playing my last season for the high school baseball squad. I'm not gaining any weight, but I can tell that my lack of physical training has made me appear weaker. Maybe this is why I am single, I begin to ponder. Then again, it's not like I am trying to date anyone right now other than Helen.

I look at my phone and see a couple of messages. Terri has been persistent. She's seems genuinely, overly worried about me. "Where are you, why haven't you called me back? I tried to send you a message on Facebook but it seems like you don't exist. What's wrong?"

Why is she so nosey? I just want to be left alone. Hell, is that not what Helen wanted? If Terri was a good friend, she would respect what her friend wants. You can't just break up with me and then expect the social interactions we share to be pleasant between me and your home girl. Then again, I really don't know what Terri wants. What do I have to lose? I guess I should call her. It is not her fault, I presume.

I go downstairs and grab a bowl of cereal in the kitchen, scavenge some fruit from the counter and venture back to my room. Using my bed as a chair, I sit up to eat breakfast and shoot Terri a text. "Yo, what's good?" I casually send and then proceed to flip my phone over hurriedly. It's like seven in the morning, I doubt Terri is even up at this time given the late timestamps of her texts from yesterday.

Surprisingly my phone begins to buzz, causing me to drop my spoon in the milk. There's no way Terri responded that quickly. But sure enough, she did. She asked if I was free today and if I wanted to meet up so we can talk. The last time someone invited me to talk, I was picking up my heart off the floor of my Honda Accord. I couldn't think of a lie fast enough, so I figured, I shouldn't. I text back that I was available, (literally and figuratively).

"Alright, great! Let's meet at the mall for lunch."

What's up with all these girls wanting to meet at the mall for lunch? Have they not heard that they serve food at other places? I don't even care to shop. But then again, those honey chicken toothpick samples are the devil. They get me every time and I always end up ordering extra egg rolls. I agree to just suck it up and deal with it. Worst case, I leave with a plate of fried rice, chicken, and egg rolls.

"Yeah, I'll be there." I reply.

I spend the next hour trying to coordinate my outfit for this impromptu lunch date. I settle for jeans and a nice shirt that Helen bought for me. I never wore it before, but with jeans it looks somewhat stylish. I still had a few hours before I needed to leave. For the first time in a while, I wasn't sad--I was more resentful now. I decide that the world has missed me long enough so it's time to re-establish a connection.

<Reactivating Facebook>

I post a status from my hiatus, "Headed out." (Corny, I know.) I tell my family that I will be back before dinner and leave before they ask any questions.

There's still plenty of time before Terri would be at the mall. I decide to canvas the area and look for some things to do to pass the time. Looking at my reflection in the rear view, I could use a haircut. I check my phone and see that I got zero likes and a string of comments on my status. All of which come from my best friends, Mark, Jesse, and Kirk. I also see that Nicole wrote on my page as well. I've known all of these people since grade school. Nicole just seems to be the only mature friend of the bunch. She writes, "Have Fun!", while my other friends use my status as a setting to practice their stand-up comedy at my expense.

"You headed out alright, big forehead boy! If you head-butted the wall, we would be homeless." - Mark

"Naw, if Aaron head-butted the Facebook wall, everyone's page would get deactivated like his was for two days." - Jesse

"You back online ain't it? About time you paid your phone bill. Can't call nobody? They make Bluetooth speakers now, you don't even have to struggle to put the phone by your ear, big head, little neck, strong breath…" - Kirk

This goes on for 10 or so more comments. I know it seems like a textbook case of cyberbullying, but this is our version of camaraderie and endearment. I reply, "Just wait until after I get back from this haircut. I'm going to light you guys up for roasting me."

Immediately Mark claps back, "Why you paying someone to cut your hair, I got this lawn mower at my house you can use for free. You need about a 24-inch blade to cover enough surface area on that big ass head you got."

I breathe a deep sigh from the light-hearted humor and walk into the barbershop that just turned on its neon "open" sign.

I put my phone in my pocket and take a seat in the chair. I say my greetings to the owners as I walk in. My usual barber is there today and was in the middle of changing the TV channel. Isaiah notices me and takes three bewildered looks at the side of my head before asking, "What are you looking to get today?"

FRIENDS, LOVERS, OR NOTHING

"Let me get a low taper and fade on the sides, keep the top a little long. Line it up all around."

"Alright, take a seat," Isaiah points towards the red leather chairs.

He begins to cut my hair and glide the clippers across my matted wig. We talk about sports for a little and debate about which team will win the super bowl this year. I tell him I am a Chargers fan and he responded, "My condolences". Of course, this guy is either one of three things, a Steelers, Cowboys, or Patriots fan--he was wearing a Tom Brady jersey as he was cutting my hair. I have very fine straight black hair, so Isaiah is tested to his limits and spends extra time not to mess up my head. I don't know why he is so nervous, I come here all the time. I think it's because I don't come as often as I should. Upon completion, I admire the masterpiece that is now my face after a new chop and slide Isaiah an extra $10 tip for his services.

I look down at my phone again and Terri texts me that she is upstairs by the food court. I could not have timed this better; I was running out of things to do. I walk towards the mall doors and proceed to follow the signs to where Terri was waiting. I manage to catch a glimpse of myself as I pass the department store mirrors. I look mad for some reason. I consciously make the choice to force a smile. The last thing I want is for anyone to pity me. Now I look ridiculous. Just be cool Aaron, be cool.

Chapter Four

Shirts and Stuff

I recognize Terri immediately from afar, she's seated alone thankfully. Her hair pinned up in a relaxed ponytail, brown hair with blonde highlights, and her natural roots had grown since graduation. She's wearing a tank top with her denim jeans and her back arched against the chair, looking around probably trying to locate me in the crowd. I walk up and wave to her, she stands up to give me a hug. The hug feels like a mannequin came to life and tackled me. This is awkward, she's never hugged me like this before. Usually she's just the third wheel or poking jabs at me like my friends. But right now, she seems delightful. Her pampered skin fills my lungs with memories of when I used to hold Helen. Helen and she must shop together for body lotions. The fragrance is identical.

"How have you been? I like your hair," Terri greeted.

"It's going well. Just been working and getting ready for school in my spare time. I leave in a few weeks for registration week."

"That's interesting. Are you nervous to be away from home?"

"Not really, I've been looking forward to college since I was a kid. I'm more excited than anything. Jesse and I are going to be roommates--so I shouldn't get too homesick."

I'm starting to get anxious, I don't understand why she was so eager for small talk. I can see why Helen and she are so close, they both like the mall's food court and like to beat around the bush.

"So, what's up, what did you want to talk about?" I blurted.

Terri squirms a little as she speaks, "I just wanted to see how you were after I heard what happened between you and Helen. I never expected you two to break up. She's talked to me about it for some time afterwards and felt like she was maybe making a mistake. I just wanted to see how you felt about it, on her behalf, and yours. I remember how happy she was to have met you. You always seemed to be able to make her laugh."

"Then why would she break up with me?" I cajole. "She kept going on about how we were too different. Yet you seem to think we were made for one another."

Terri seems to be wanting to shed a few tears herself. I can read her mind from her facial expressions. Her lips are on the edge of saying, "I'm so sorry."

"If you are wondering how I feel, I feel broken. I can feel my heart palpitate when you mention her name. I spent the last two years of high school walking beside her to and from classes with every intention of spending the next four years racing back and forth on weekends to visit her. For me nothing has changed." I protest.

"But how do you think she was going to feel waiting days on end just to see you leave again? You don't think she wanted more for herself?" Terri points out.

"Obviously. But what do you want me to say? Of course, I wish for her to be happy. That's the goal of a relationship, isn't it? I desperately hope she finds happiness, because otherwise both of us will be unhappy. I was willing to try out this long-distance relationship, it's not my fault she would rather stay here. She's way smarter than me. Either I put my goals on hold and limit my options or lose her. Staying here would have just postponed the inevitable." I try to selflessly defend.

(I guess this is my fault anyways. I would be selfish to think Helen should only be happy with me. If Terri is looking for a happy ending, now isn't the time. I'm not going to hurt myself, I'm already hurting. There's no need for me to be redundant. I just don't see myself wanting anything, anymore.)

"I didn't know you cared for her like that, and I'm sorry to hear you are unhappy," Terri empathizes.

"Forever was a long time, and three days ago it ended," I scoff and manage to say without crying. I guess I could not hide my emotions no matter how hard I tried.

FRIENDS, LOVERS, OR NOTHING

Terri seemed to be content with my response. I seemed discontent with my own response. I haven't told a soul what I've been going through these past couple days. I never even told Nicole and she deserves to know. But I'm afraid to tell her because she would be the first to throw me a pity party or the first to call me asking for bail money. At this moment, neither option would be beneficial. Truthfully, I wanted to talk to Terri because I know what I say will get back to Helen. My pride would not let me call Helen myself to plead my case; but I have no problem using Terri as a surrogate. Terri and I chat for a few more minutes unrelated to Helen. She hugs me goodbye, but this time, I am not reminded of Helen's fragrance. I can actually feel a sense that Terri seemed hopeful for me. Similarly, she asks me to make her a promise to call her sometime. In the most platonic way, I agree and we part ways. I manage to grab a box of the honey chicken to go on my way out to eat while in my car. I wonder what Terri is going to say to Helen.

I get to my car in the parking garage and look down at my phone to check my Facebook. I am greeted with memes of my face photo shopped over a landscaping ad stylized with a barbershop quartet. I've neglected my friends for far too long and they clearly had the time today to keep the roast session active. While I was bleeding my heart out to Terri, these folks have been having a bloodbath on my social media wall as to who could be the most vicious roaster.

"Jesse, you look like a killer whale minus the ocean. Mark, your nose is so big you were able to smell the future and see this comment coming. Kirk, my bad I did not call you--I was too busy stealing those ketchup packets from McDonald's you requested. You still need them to make sandwiches, right?" I quickly jab back to them on Facebook. After finishing my food, I start scrolling through my contacts to call Nicole.

Before I could hit dial, Helen's face appears on my screen. I'm numb and powerless again. I don't even remember bringing the phone to my ear. She whispers hello. For some reason I can envision that she is laying on her bed, wearing denim shorts, and one of my anime t-shirts just from the sound of her voice. I say "Hey…" followed by a long-expected amount of silence.

"I still have a bunch of your stuff. I don't want to throw it away—do you want me to bring it by?" Helen asks.

(For goodness sakes! Drive the knife and turn it clockwise, why don't you? Thanks for helping a brother out, Terri. I haven't been gone 20 minutes and it seems that our conversation has already been relayed.)

"Sure, just come by later today if you want," I actually say.

"Okay, bye…" she says, as I keep the phone pressed to my ear long after the call ends.

Her face disappears from my screen and the display returns to my list of contacts. Nicole's name is still highlighted. But before I could remember what I needed to call her about—I start forming a list in my mind of all the items Helen could possibly be trying to return. It's probably just a bunch of t-shirts and stuffed animals. I could make use of the jackets I lent her over the years, the vintage t-shirts, and those hats I bought on clearance. (Having a weird shaped head has its benefits). What the hell am I going to do with a bunch of stuffed animals?

Chapter Five

The Last Time

<You're listening to 101.5 FM Soul and Disco radio; up next we have the classic hit 'Smokey Robinson – Cruising'> - DJ Love Heart screams from the radio while scratching the music in from a low fade.

Why did the soul station hire such an eccentric person? Shouldn't it be some deep baritone voiced smooth jazz aficionado? "Today just keeps getting stranger," I think to myself as I turn up the radio. I love this song by the way, it always brings me back to earth. Especially at a time like this where my mind is racing to see Helen and my heart keeps skipping beats. I think about the first time Helen and I met as I drove away from the mall. I seem to catch every red light. God must be asking me to slow down and think about her even more.

Helen was older than me by a few months, wiser than me by a few years, but her beauty seemed timeless. I was the chubby kid in the class that cracked jokes all the time to make up for my lack of athletic ability. I focused on developing my personality and sharpening my intellect. Yes, I am a nerd. This was at least 3 years before we started dating. The golden years before hormones intoxicated our minds, before the brand names mattered, and before genetics differentiated you from the lot of ugly ducklings. We were all close friends but for some reason Helen hated the sight of me. (I blame it on the crude social complex that men can't rationalize their emotions, so we choose to insult instead of compliment. This logic doesn't apply well when courting the ladies and my inner circle has yet to learn to do otherwise either.)

Helen would look pass me as if my parents were glass makers. But one day, I tried to compliment Helen on her new hair style. She normally wore it back in a single braided ponytail. On this particular day, her long thick, blonde hair carefully cradled against the flat side of her shoulder blades. You could see her neck was encased by the cascading strands of shadows made by her relaxed hair. She had clearly straightened it and took pride in her efforts. I told her that she looked really nice. She responded, "Go to hell, Aaron." Instinctively, I said, "As long as you aren't there. Sure!" I remember her blushing transformed her frowning face to a slight smirk, revealing the outline of her dental braces.

The year after, we would no longer be in the same class because of the transition to high school. She decided to avoid taking any more college preparatory classes; I maintained and stuck it out with the same cohort of people that I met during junior high. She didn't have to deal with my incessant jokes during class anymore, I was free from her side eye rolls and flabbergasted sighs. I start to regret ever falling in love with her as I reminisce. Because now I was falling back in love with her all over again. We were just two different people with too different goals. Was I wrong to write her that silly poem that sparked our relationship? I did so on a whim just to let her know I noticed she got her braces removed. Who knew that those words scribbled on a sheet of notebook paper would challenge our feuding friendship?

"Helen,

Your smile has always been pretty. I notice your braces are gone. Hopefully you can now stop being so gritty, for all the things I've done wrong.

Sincerely,

Your favorite resident of Hell."

We went from ignoring one another, to having lunch together, then having extended phone calls late into the evening, nearly every evening. From there I was writing countless letters to pass in between class periods in the hallway. We were each other's first love.

Now the radio was silent when I finally do make it home. The sun was ready to set and the fireflies were beginning to emerge. The faint sounds of frogs and crickets in the background echo during a half visible moon's glare, accompanied by resonating minutes of silence from my calming heart. I look at my phone and see that Nicole has called me twice. I must have inadvertently kept it on silent during lunch with Terri. I'm not ready to speak with her just yet. Now, I remember that I was going to finally tell her about Helen and I breaking up.

Nicole was neither a fan nor a foe of Helen's. Nicole was a fan of Aaron, me. She was one of the only girls to ever get my humor from day one and could appreciate the brevity my friends and I brought to classroom. There were plenty of mean girls to go around high school, but Nicole was probably the nicest of the mean girls (if there is such a thing). She didn't have to talk about you to make you look foolish, she just ignored you in a way where you felt incompetent. Yet, I was her close friend. She told me that I was original and never tried to judge anyone. Everyone else was faking it to make it. In a way, we looked out for each other because she knows I'm actually quite the sensitive person underneath my facade.

"Sorry, I have been really busy. Can I call you back later tonight?" I sincerely text Nicole.

"Of course! We need to catch up. Don't become brand new just because you are leaving for school!"

Brand new? Humph. She's silly. If only she knew the truth, it would seem that I'm the only one around here who hasn't changed. I make my way into the house and speak to my parents. My dad is sitting at the kitchen table watching videos on his tablet. He's chuckling to himself while watching some overseas game show. My mother is finishing up a phone call with my aunt. She seems to not notice me or my new haircut. I make my way up the stairs into my room, walking past the empty bedrooms of my older brothers. They must be at work or out with their friends. I stand in front of my bedroom and stare at the decorations from the door. My solid oak bed frame, matching nightstands, and computer desk make up the bulk of my furniture options. There is a tiny closet with a dresser adjacent to the doorway. Most of my clothes are off the hangers. My new computer purchase is still unopened in the middle of the room. There are a few open boxes along the wall with the items I need to bring with me to college. I press my hand against the semi-gloss yellow painted walls. I recall how I painted my room last year per suggestion from Helen. She always felt that the bland, off-white walls were too moot. I chose a bright-matte yellow called "solar fusion". She was not a fan at first and was surprised I chose anything outside of blue or gray. But secretly, every time I walk into my room it reminds me of that day I first complimented Helen. Drawing the conclusion that most of my decisions have revolved around her since we've been together. "Who am I without her?" I ponder.

I stop daydreaming to tidy up my room before Helen arrives. I don't expect us to have a long conversation, but you never know. I definitely did not have the closure I needed from our last conversation. She may be here to tell me it was all nerves and she was overreacting. What if she is just here to drop off some things? What will I say? I want to be with her, but I am not compelled to fight for her. I have watched too many romance films with Helen to ignore their advice, "If you love them, let them go; if they come back, that's how you know". I was on the fence on whether or not this situation applies. The other side of me wants to just be left alone, but I rationalize that I have the rest of my life to be alone. Now is the time to say what needs to be said. I can't give up just yet; I'm not ready to let go.

I fix the sheets on my bed. I set aside the pictures of Helen and I around my room. I want to remove any impression that a makeshift shrine was being built. She did break up with me, but she didn't break my sanity. I slide the empty bowl of cereal from this morning underneath the bed. I look in the mirror and make sure that my hair did not suddenly regrow to its original length from this morning. I can feel my heart this time. I can hear it beating, pounding, and pushing against the cavity in my chest. I'm nervous. I feel as if we are meeting for the first time, for the last time.

Chapter Six

Divine

Helen arrives as my parents were leaving for a date. Even after 25 years, my parents still found the time to go out and enjoy themselves. I bet they are just going to catch a movie and dinner. My parents still do not know that Helen and I broke up, so we pretend to save face and act like nothing's changed when Helen comes through the door. My dad tells me to make sure I lock the door if we decide to leave, since I'm the only one home. I grab the box that Helen is carrying and set it on the coffee table in the living room. The box feels surprisingly light. The box is from a blender that I bought for Helen last Valentine's Day. (Look, I never said I knew what women wanted, but this was on sale and she actually uses it.)

She looks around my house and seems to be comfortable. She takes a seat on the far end of the couch as I begin to open the box. She looks away as I lift the flaps up on the box to uncover the contents. There's a tin makeup box, some hats, and a few shirts (far less than I expected). No stuffed animals in sight. I open the makeup box to see that it's a pile of letters. A stack of previously folded sheets of paper with my handwriting. Each sheet was chronologically sorted, organized with paper clips, and photos attached to a few inserts. There has to be at least one hundred pages alone here. I don't think I could even locate all the letters that Helen wrote me. I don't know what to say, but I look up at Helen and realize the magnitude of the time we have spent together.

"Why are you giving these to me?" I inquire as I push them back towards her.

"I figured you'd want them. And I don't want to throw any of them away. You spent a lot of time writing these," responds Helen.

"But you manage to keep the jackets I lent you?" I question.

"You *gave* those to me." She sarcastically says.

"I also *gave* you these letters, but here you are trying to return them. A man has arms, too, and these goose bumps don't discriminate. I could make use of those jackets. I can't burn these letters for much warmth."

(Helen laughs.)

"I also gave you my heart, will you be returning that as well, Helen? It's not in the box, nor is the blender." I protest.

Helen looks away. "I didn't come here for that, Aaron. I just wanted to bring you these. You said we would still be friends, don't tell me you lied to me," Helen repeats.

"Don't make me lie to you. Do you really want to be just friends? This was never a really real choice for me. I don't even know what's wrong. This is not going to be easy. We

30

were together for two years. I feel like we are still together now," I say.

"It's hard for me, too. But this is for the best. I know you'll be alright," Helen predicts to me.

"Are you sure, you'll be alright? I can wait forever if you asked me to, but don't expect a notebook of letters at your door," I allude.

　　She stares at me with the same eyes from when we last spoke. Before she could reply, I grab a random sheet out of the stack of notes. I read it, taking a gamble as to which memories it would invoke. Dated a year ago written in my archaic chicken scratch called penmanship:

Divine

"I remember how you once told me my kiss was sweeter than wine, does that mean without a sip, the pleasure accentuates with time?

If so, let's fast forward to then when I'm ripe in the present and you can indulge into my soul and taste the missed resin.

I've said before that you have a galore outpoured from heaven. And not for a moment have I lost sense of your perfection.

I reach out to feel your lips pout, I reminisce being without. Often the memory of how I'm held close to your soft skin.

I grow in circles to help fulfill the purpose of your thirst, unlimited source of passion, purple adjacent to the earth.

Bruised are others, but I refuse to stop being your destined lover, or at least taste this good to future connoisseurs.

It is from you I breathe in truth of the air, you bring the water to my spirit and replenish.

Life's goodness is first distributed by your mention."

"I wrote these words for you Helen. For me, it's never been a fantasy. I've always thought of you. I'm sorry if I haven't been there for you, but I don't want to be without-"

Before I could finish speaking, Helen grabs my face and knocks the stack of papers to the floor. She kisses me to shut me up. I nonchalantly fight it because my pride refuses to succumb to pity, but my body easily surrenders. She's not crying like I was expecting. I open my eyes and see her glare intently into my pupils. No longer transparent to my emotions, she holds the side of my jaw. This isn't pity. This was the familiar love that nourished me throughout these last few years. I look back at her and count the freckles on her face. Every inch of her skin is smooth with a light coat of foundation. Her lips glisten with a glossy pink rose colored smear. I resist her advances at first but her intoxicating fragrance compels me to return her affections. I lost count of the amount of time that has passed. At this point, she has pushed me back into the couch. My shoulders firmly pinned to the arm of the furniture. Her fingers laced around my hand, she is a few inches from my face. She whispers, "I missed you so much." I repeat her words immediately with more emphasis. She beckons me to my own room. I give chase as our footsteps echo throughout my empty home.

We may or may not have done the "do". And if it did happen, it definitely lasted longer than 3 minutes. That's a new personal record. Afterwards, Helen and I look up at the stars outside my window while lying together in my bed. Her medium sized frame sheltered in my arms, I inhale the smell of her shampoo as I pressed my nose on the back of her hair. She holds my hand in hers and casually caresses the skin around my wrists. This moment is surreal; I can feel that her skin has dampened from our spontaneous adventure. I turn her to face me, she smiles. My heart is now fluttering, a sensation of energy rushes to my skin. My goodness how I cherish this woman. She is divine.

Chapter Seven

Change My Mind

Sunday morning, I wake up alone. Helen left last night, leaving the letters in my possession. I made sure to collect them all from the living room floor before anyone could notice the box. They would be disappointed to see it didn't actually contain a blender. I didn't sleep very much at all; I was so relieved to have reconnected with Helen. I check my phone to see if there were any messages. There were none. I reread the messages Helen used to notify that she arrived home safely. Sure enough, the texts were real; last night was not a dream.

I have to go to church in a few hours with my family. This is one of the last few weekends before I go off to college. For my father, these moments are very important to him. He's been praying for one of us to graduate college for as long as I can remember. He never had the option to pursue higher education. He's been a laborer all his life. My summer gig came through his company and I was able to experience, firsthand, the toils of his occupation. It has made me look forward to sitting in a desk and reading a book all day.

After my shower, I put on my formal clothes. Black slacks, collared dress shirt, blue tie, silver looped belt, and black shoes. I adjust my fit in the mirror and think about the person

I wish to become one day. Am I looking at the future me? I feel as if I am staring at a clone from another dimension. These clothes are an anomaly to my usual work attire of casual clothes. I don't dress up too often. I look like I park cars for a living. I would wear a jacket but the weather is still too hot for that. I suddenly remember that I forgot to call Nicole back yesterday. I feel terrible, but I know she will understand. The phone rings twice before I can hear her cheery voice.

"About time you called me! Where have you been? Mark and them are so ignorant. They spent at least 4 hours on your page roasting you." Nicole greets.

"Yeah, those guys are hilarious. I have just been too busy with work and all. I've been meaning to call you to talk to you about something, but I don't think it's important anymore."

"Oh, that's expected. We both have to save our own money for school now you know? We are grown! Can you believe it? Our parents can't tell us what to do anymore. I wish we were going to the same school, but you know I'll always keep in touch no matter where you are," Nicole tells me.

"I hope so. The internet makes it easy. I'm always on my phone anyways--so it shouldn't be hard to reach me." I reply.

"So, what _did_ you want to talk about? How are you and Helen doing?" She asks innocently.

"That's kind of what I wanted to talk to you about, but it seems like we are doing fine now. She actually broke up with

me a few days ago; but I guess we are back together now." I
finally admit to Nicole.

"What do you mean she *broke up* with you? What do you
mean you guess you are *back together* now? Why did you take
her back? Am I on speakerphone?" She quickly queries and
interrogates me.

(I'm not sure how to prioritize my responses.)

"Well the other day, she and I broke up at the mall. She told
me things like, 'we are too different, we aren't meant to be',
blah blah blah. I take it that she was upset at the thought of
us being apart for the first time since we've been together. But
last night she came over and we, you know, talked it out over a
nice cup of tea." I lie.

"You... talked it out? Did that involve you wearing clothes?!"
Nicole wittingly dissects.

"We...may have... done some things. But that is beside the
point. I professed to her that I didn't want to lose her, then
one thing led to another, and we are good now. We are good,"
I defend.

"That doesn't sound good to me. If I break up with someone,
there is a good reason for it. I don't think words are enough
to fix the underlying problem. You don't even know what she
means by you all are so different. You may want her back, but
you don't need her back. If she was willing to leave you in the

36

first place, something is not right." Nicole points out a very good hypothesis.

"I know what you are saying, but Helen just needed some space. I think it worked itself out." I hopefully reply.

"If you say so, but don't be surprised if she changes her mind again. I don't know Helen as well as I know you, but I know that we women tend to be indecisive. And being miles apart is going to provide her with plenty of time to think. Did you at *least* pull out?!"

Oh lord… Nicole has never been one to bite her tongue, Sunday is no exception.

"I'm not fooling with you today, Nicole! Ha. I'll let you know how things turn out. Sooner next time, too. I promise. And we need to meet up with the rest of the crew one more time before school starts for us."

"Agreed! Alright then. I will talk to you later, don't try to keep things to yourself too much. Bye." Nicole delightfully ends our call.

I finish getting dressed by tying my shoes and head downstairs to meet the rest of my family. We load up into the truck and drive a few miles down the street to our church. I watch the many families congregate near the entrance of the chapel. People are fellowshipping with one another and everyone seems to be delighted. We all have something to be thankful for this morning. I exit the truck and head towards the crowd with my hands in my pocket. I count the number of couples in front of us and compare them to the number of single faces. Most of the ones my age are grouped together. I start to think of Helen because I rather be with her right now. But Nicole's words are still resonating the back of my mind. Something's not right.

Chapter Eight

Love Her More

Walking pass the volunteers handing out the itineraries for today's sermon, I make my way to the usual pews located near the top of the stairs. My family shuffles beside me and we line up accordingly. I read the program in my hand and try to determine how far we have to go before service is over. As the remaining parishioners settle down to their seats, the choir is bringing the hymn to a close. Pastor Stone steps up to the stage, microphone over his chin, gleefully smiling as he approaches the podium.

"Joyful is the day that the Lord has made… Amen church?" Pastor Stone hypes us.

"Amen!" the congregation resounds.

"Today we have a very special occasion. I know many of us are preparing for college in the coming weeks and many of us are going to be delighted to have these kids finally out the house. Amen?"

"AMEN!" a roar of parents screams, some even already broke into dance as if they have caught the spirit. There is laughter throughout the room, my parents are staring at me while my brothers are shaking me by my shoulders.

"Settle down, settle down church. All jokes aside, it is a blessing to see our children grow and become outstanding citizens. So today, I wanted us to be able to reflect on the relationships forged through God's love and His guidance that brought us here. To pray that His Will, shall continue to carry us forward. I ask Deacon Smith to lead us in prayer to open up service." Pastor Stone hands a microphone over to Deacon Smith.

"Heavenly Father, we thank you for this day. This beautiful Sunday morning and wonderful weather that you have provided us. We pray that you continue to protect us and forgive us of our sins. We pray that you guide Pastor Stone in delivering your message to the full extent of your Word, O Lord. I pray that you resolve those speeding tickets from last June that I have yet to pay. If you can find it in your heart to provide the funds to our peppermint candy budget and bless the congregation that needs it most; it may take a miracle, but Lord we know you are capable. We pray that those children who are heading off to college don't become addicted to the drugs, the sex, the alcohol, and the partying like I was when I was younger, Father… I pray they don't learn just how *easy* it is to never go to class and still manage to pass school, if you just study two hours before the test. We pray they become diligent and we thank you for your love… Amen."

"AMEN." The church echoes.

The church lifts their heads from prayer. I look around and wonder if I am the only person that heard Deacon Smith's prayer. Everyone seems to be focused intently on Pastor Stone as he cuts on his mic.

"The value of a relationship is clearly demonstrated with the covenant of Jesus's love for mankind. It is that bond that brings us the capability to be able to come to God and be absolved from sin, for whoever so believes in Him--shall have eternal life! But what about other relationships mentioned in the bible? What does the Word mention on how relationships can bring us closer to God? We can look to examples of brotherhood, lovers, and enemies in the bible and translate its relevance to present day struggles." Pastor Stone opens the sermon with such passion.

"There's the relationship of Cain and Abel. Brothers vying for God's blessing that later turns into the first murder in human history, sparking the vampire book genre. Then you have the story of Abraham and Sarah. A bond of love forged by sheer will and faith. Although Sarah did mess off and lose faith for a little bit, she eventually came back to her senses…" Pastor Stone now begins to go on a tangent...

I doze in and out of consciousness to eventually be awakened to the collection plate slide sliding across my lap. I look up and see Pastor Stone stretch his arms wide to ask those with heaviness on their heart to come forward. People gravitate to the altar to ask for either forgiveness or to provide a testimony. They then line up by the side door and are escorted off to be counseled by ministers. The choir is singing a melodically strung with the lyrics "come as you are, heaven can heal." As the music begins to silence, the lights dim and a spotlight is shined at the baptismal pool above the stage.

There is a woman standing there in a white gown. She reminds me of Helen. She is tall with long blondish hair and a face filled with conviction. She smiles as Pastor Stone asks us to stand as we bear witness to her proclaimed dedication. He holds her face and supports her back as she is submerged into the water. When she erupts from the pool, the congregation is applauding her commitment. Eyes everywhere begin to become teary and there is a moment of grace that captures the church. I rise to clap as well. I pan the room and my fear of being alone fades. I read the bottom of the program.

"Trust in the Lord with all your heart, and do not lean on your own wisdom. In all your ways acknowledge him, and he will straighten your paths."

I have a moment of serendipity. I have been so focused on Helen this week that I haven't attempted to prioritize the things that I can control. I leave in less than two weeks for college. Will I be able to handle being away from home? How will these pews feel with one less person sitting there? I am just beginning to regain control of my emotions. I don't like knowing that my composure is dependent on things out of my hands. Service ends and we funnel towards the opened exits. I get in the truck and check my phone, noticing three new messages.

"I love you." - Helen

"Still coming over to get beat in Street Fighter?" - Mark

"Have you decided on a major? What do we need for our dorms?" - Jesse

Oh yeah, I do need to kick it with Mark, today. I text him that I should be able to make it there in a few hours. My family and I are headed out to eat lunch together immediately after service. I also tell Jesse that I am still undecided about my major and we will talk at Mark's house. That's just something I need to sit down and think about more. I stare back at the first text from Helen. Reflecting on the experiences of this past hour, I know exactly what to say. "I love you more."

Chapter Nine

Long Way to Go

I pack my bag for the afternoon. I change out of my church clothes to put on something more casual. I don't expect us to do much beside chill and play video games. I've known Mark, Jesse, and Kirk for well over 7 years. They have been there for the good and bad days I shared with Helen. When Helen and I started dating, I would split my time between both groups. Sometimes we would try to all group date, but Terri and Mark never saw eye to eye again after their short-stinted relationship fizzled. Mark comes off as a goof, but he is an undercover heartbreaker. He does not invest his emotions as deeply as I do. Mark slept with Terri, she became attached, and it was all kinds of bad from there. Then I remember Kirk tried to talk to Terri. Terri didn't give him the time of day just because of association. Speaking of Kirk, I need to see what his plans are tonight. I text Kirk to see if he was going to be over Mark's house.

"Kirk, you going to be able to come to Mark's house today?" I ask.

"Nah, bro. I got me a date today. I have to get ready to pick her up. I will catch up with you before you leave though." - Kirk

"I see you still out there chasing tail, you know that you aren't cute right? You might as well come over and quit wasting your time. Just tell her you don't date crazy people." I reply.

"How do you know if she is crazy or not?" Kirk asks.

"Because she's letting you take her out on a date. Duh!" I joke.

"Ha, yeah yeah. While you all at home playing video games, I'm going to be playing the real game. Playa, Playa!" Kirk responds.

I roll up to Mark's house and see that Jesse has already slid his way there. I walk in and say hello to his folks and his mother gives me a hug. She asks me if I'm hungry and forces a slice of sweet potato pie to me. It is as delicious as it smells.

"What's up, Aaron? Where your big forehead been hiding? I heard there was an earthquake in California, did you hit your head on the ground or something?" Mark says as he comes over to give me dap.

"Nah man, I have not been hiding." I would normally return the jokes, but his mother is standing beside me. You can't just insult the child of the woman's hand that fed you.

"Hey Aaron, is that you over there eating all the sweet potato pie? Can I press some of these yams across your forehead so we can hurry up and make some more?" Jesse confidently chimes in with a bead of sweat across his brow.

"I'll be glad to Jesse, just let me swim over to where you are right now." I quickly retort.

Jesse wasn't Mark's real brother, so he is fair game to get roasted. Jesse doesn't believe in antiperspirant, so he ends up sweating all the time. We each have a fatal flaw that we embrace. My big forehead, Mark's industrial vacuum nose, Jesse's sweaty nature, and Kirk's immovable resolve for rejection. Why are we friends? Because no matter how much we rag on one another, we will always stick up for each other. Whenever Terri and Mark broke up, she tried to talk bad about him on Facebook. Terri had gone as far as to post up private conversations they shared and clown him on the internet for cheap likes. Kirk and Jesse responded with so many ruthless memes, "but you let him hit though!" The block button could not have been pressed sooner. Helen didn't allow me to join in on the fun and that's why Terri is still unknowingly cool with me. I had much of my own material lined up to post, too.

There's a knock at the front door. We all walk up to see that Kirk did manage to make it over. He was overdressed compared to the rest of us. He was wearing designer jeans, a dark polo shirt, and cheap sunglasses. We all were surprised to see him there especially after he said he wasn't going to be able to make it. He walks in with a jovial mood and follows us back into the kitchen.

"Kirk! What you doing here man? I thought you was on a date." Mark opens up the conversation.

"Nah man, I decided to swing over here instead, I realize Aaron was not going to be here in a few weeks so we need to hang out while we all can," Kirk responds.

"That girl stood you up, didn't she?" Mark says without pause.

"Naw, I was able to see her. I just dropped her off at the movies and left afterwards." Kirk says.

"What do you mean you left afterwards? How is she going to get home?" Jesse asks with a raised eyebrow. You can see the sweat roll down the side of his face now.

"I'm sure the guy that she went to see the movie with will be able to drop her off at home." Kirk says in a hurry.

A strange silence fills the kitchen. You can literally hear Mark's nose stop breathing.

"You mean to tell us, you *picked* her up and *gave* her a ride to be able to go on a date with *another dude*? Did she at least give you gas money?" I comment.

We all start laughing and even Mark's mother chimes in at the exact right moment. "You need some sweet potato pie, baby?"

"Naw momma, he needs some milk! This boy ain't a man. He just the driver." Mark says while his sides are splitting.

FRIENDS, LOVERS, OR NOTHING

We then head towards the back of the house where we intend to hangout. Mark already has a game loaded up in the console and Jesse hands me the controller. As we hover on the character select screen, my phone vibrates in my pocket. Work emailed us our final schedule for the week. I will now be working first shift and there is a company luncheon planned for all the college bound interns on Friday. I also see that Helen has updated her profile picture to our prom photo. Jesse selects his character in Street Fighter, I hover over the character, Charlie, while shooting Helen a text.

"At Mark's right now, text me when you are free. My schedule for work changed so let's make more plans to spend time together." I send to Helen.

Helen replies almost immediately with a smiley face. "I'll be home in a few hours. Have fun, babe."

We all huddle around the television screen staring intently as the match carries on. I execute a few combos on Jesse that he was not prepared for. Ten seconds later, the match is over. Jesse throws his controller across the room and screams, "Man… Fuck Charlie!" The controller is drenched in sweat. I pass the sticks to Kirk, who smells like a bottle of rubbing alcohol. His "cologne" is essentially half a can of body spray. Mark takes over for Jesse and we all spend the evening hanging out for what seems like a last good measure. Kirk begins his match with some words to top off the evening.

"I know we are always going to be friends and brothers. It's so strange to know that in a week, two of us will be going off the school in another city. I wish we all could go together." Kirk tearfully says.

"Are you crying?" Mark asks.

"Nah I just sprayed some cologne in my eye by accident." Kirk denies.

"Good, don't be crying up in my room and getting all sentimental. What does it look like for a bunch of dudes to be crying over one another? You don't see me crying over these girls. I'm not going to be crying with you." Mark proudly says.

"I think what Mark means to say, Kirk, is 'don't worry too much.' We've been together this far, we still have a long way to go," I conclude.

My night at Mark's ends a few hours later when Helen texts me she is free to talk. I gather my things and head out. We do the customary handshakes then bounce. I let them know I'll be back in town often to kick it. Mark's mom packed me a slice of pie to take home with me as I walk back to my car. I call Helen from my car and drive home. She answers and I naturally say, "Hey babe, how was your day been?"

Chapter Ten

Genesis

The week starts off as it usually does. Scratch that. It's quite unusual because every day this week, I've spent time with Helen. It's as if we fell in love again for the second time. Monday after work, I pay money to sit in a movie theatre just to miss every scene. My hands get tangled as my fingers comb through her thick, vibrant hair. I can make out the patterns in her eyes as they shimmer and reflect the panning of the projector light. There isn't a soul in this theatre to witness us lose ourselves in each other's embrace. I whisper to her sweet nothings in between each kiss; she giggles and wondrously listens on. She gives me that look from Saturday night. We may or may not have left extra butter on the popcorn tonight.

Tuesday, Helen and I hang out at my house. I have my new laptop open on my bed. I am laying down, chest forward, reviewing courses trying to plot out my next four academic years. She is laying on the curve of my lower back. Chemistry? Biology? Calculus? So many classes to take, I tense up from the stress. Helen scoots forward and rests her cheek on my shoulder. "You got it babe," she reassures me. I close the laptop and we hypothetically plan our future together. She tells me how much she'll miss me. I listen to colors of a wedding she envisioned since she was a little girl. We talk about her goals. We fall asleep embracing one another surrounded by my packed room.

On Wednesday, we all kick it. Helen and I meet with Terri and my guys at the bowling alley. Terri would normally not agree to this but she did it out of consideration for me. Terri is obviously flirting with Kirk, while Mark pays no attention. Mark knows she is still crazy about him, but he is not the jealous type. Nicole and Mark are just laughing together as Jesse walks up to bowl his turn. Kirk signals to me that he may get lucky tonight. I profusely shake my head side to side to warn him not to get his hopes up. Jesse is bowling terribly as he is unable to grip the ball effectively. The ball keeps sliding off his hands into the gutter. Jesse screams profanity after each failed attempt, we all laugh. Helen is seated beside me with her adorable bowling shoes tucked on top of the bench seats. Her head planted under my arm again as we both look onto our silly friends' antics. By the end of the evening, we take one last picture together to memorialize our final summer as kids.

Thursday, Helen takes me shopping at the mall. I try on a multitude of outfits. She is clearly enjoying this more than I am. I take this opportunity to showcase my runway skills. She laughs at the expressions on my face. With each wardrobe change, I commit deeper into the modeling showcase hidden in the dressing room hallway. The more Helen laughs, the more I embrace the character. Eventually, I lose face and we are neck high in discarded clothes that don't make the cut. By the end of it all, I settle for only a few outfits. Most of the apparel I select are jackets to replace the ones that Helen has claimed.

Friday comes and it's the last day at the job. I'm surrounded by my fellow peers that are also off to start their college journeys. Ms. Jones is tearfully hugging me and wishing me the best. The teammates from my assembly line are enjoying the free cake and food from the company. I realize that this place has provided me more than just extra income, it has given me insight on my future. No matter where you are headed, never forget where you've been. My parents are there as well to share in the delightful pleasantries. It is the first time I have seen my folks cry in regards to me leaving for school. The mood is quite bittersweet.

Saturday arrives as quickly as it is over. My parents go to sleep early so they can be well rested to help me move into my dorm. They don't know that Helen is spending the night with me. Helen knows I will be leaving for school tomorrow. We hide in my room for the evening, I lock my door to keep my brothers from barging in accidentally. Even though we are somewhat adults now, Helen and I masquerade around wildly in this teenage love affair.

Helen looks remarkable tonight. Her makeup is applied flawlessly. The mascara on her eyelashes is perfectly applied with detailed precision. The dimples in her cheeks are lightly coated with a blanket of powdery blush and her perfume lightly fills the atmosphere of my room. She moves her long hair back around her earlobe. She shows off a pair of earrings that I got her for her birthday earlier this year. She is wearing a light cream satin shirt to complement her indigo hip-hugging jeans. I pull her close by her waist and she chortles as her frame falls closer to me. I grab her hand and rub my thumb purposefully around her ring finger. She knows I love her deeply, but we are not quite ready for that step. I slightly turn up my laptop volume for the music to mask our noises. She turns off the lights and allows me to trace her silhouette in the dark. We spend the evening rewriting the book of Genesis.

Chapter Eleven

First Impressions

Sunday morning comes and the big day has finally here. I pretend to open the door for Helen to make it seem that she just arrived. My parents are up cooking breakfast and my brothers are loading things into the car for me. Once my mother has finished preparing the food, we all gather in the kitchen to eat. My father prays so long that the food begins to get cold. After eating we gather around the car. Helen hugs me and sheds a few tears. I wipe them away and remind her that she can visit me as often as she likes, and that I will be back as often as I can. She nods her head.

Helen knows she will be busy with her own engagements as well. She just received an offer to be an admin for a retail outlet store. She is excited to start training and loves the idea of being able to get an employee discount and having her own money. She has the knack for fashion and is a delight to be around--so I am sure she will be just fine while I am face deep in my studies. I realize that it's not just a one-sided affair. As much as I would love for her to come with me to college, she would love for me to stay here. But if last night was any sort of a covenant, I know that we owe it to each other to at least test the limits of this relationship. We both get into our cars and prepare to drive our separate paths. Before I can even lose sight of my house,

Helen texts me, "I miss you already. Can't wait to see you this weekend."

My college is about two hours away from home. The drive is filled with pastures of farmland, sporadic small towns, and no need to stop for fuel. Throughout the drive, I reflect on whether this college was the right decision. Ultimately, I want to embed my career in the health field. The advantages to choosing the college was their in-network effect with the health professions graduate school. Aside from that, I didn't even bother to do much investigating on the surrounding areas of my college. I put my faith on the academic requirements and set aside any social offerings other schools promote. School for me was just one milestone, I do not need to pursue non-essential interactions. A part of me also enjoys the fact that I will be only a few hours away from home. I knew I would eventually get homesick; I just wasn't expecting it to be this soon.

I approach the archways that bridge the small town and the campus. Driving by the hordes of parked cars and fellow residents currently moving in to their dorms. I try to capture all of the activity going on. There are so many unknowns faces, strangers, and intricate happenings that I am mentally trying to resolve from my vantage point. I no longer feel like I am the smartest person in the room. I am lost and have not even taken my seatbelt off. Jesse told me he was already here, so hopefully he has an idea of what is the next step. My email says Sunday is get Settled Day. Move-in, eat dinner at the café in the student union, and learn the lay of the land. Tomorrow begins R.O.A.R. week (Registration, Outreach, Academic Research), designed to help freshmen adjust to being college students. Official classes start next week on Monday, so it's best to do this before the upperclassman return. I count well over three thousand people in the crowd, spread across the green lush fields surrounding the dormitories.

I put my things on a bellhop cart and push my tiny world gallantly down the halls of my dorm. (Martin Hall, my future home for the next 4 years.) I locate my door, insert my room key, and with a slight turn, open it to reveal Jesse standing there with open arms in his underwear. The room is freezing cold. I can hear that the air conditioner is on its max setting.

"Hey Aaron! Welcome Home… I made dinner!" Jesse reveals an open box of cereal.

"Well, at least he isn't sweating." I think to myself.

Jesse helps me get my things together and he pushes the cart down the hall into the wall. I fix my sheets on the twin mattress, set up my desk, hang the clothes (some with tags still on them), and see that Helen managed to sneak her tin box of letters into my box. I place the letters in a drawer in my desk.

Jesse already staked his claim of which side of the room he wanted, so I ended up closer to the front of room by the door. His bed is closer to the air conditioner. I doubt it helps his situation. I take a selfie with my side of the room in the background to send to my family and Helen.

"That's the cleanest I've ever seen your room!" love Mom & Dad.

"Is that my side of the bed? Which part of the floor is yours?" Helen asks.

I reply, "We will figure that out when you come here to visit."

I check my watch to see that it is almost time for dinner. Jesse gets dressed in a white tank top and basketball shorts. I put on a t-shirt and fix my hair in the mirror. I haven't eaten since breakfast.

We get to the university center and line up in the crowd of people by the cafe. It's like high school, except everyone is isolated at the moment. We just try to create small talk with the people around us. The cliques have yet to form. I meet one guy named Ellis, he looks like he lifts weights and likes to eat. He happens to also be from Memphis. What a small world. He sits with us at the dinner table. Tonight's buffet banquet is provided by the University. We have over ten plates spread across the table for the three of us. A few more people decide to join us and we begin to share stories. So far, college isn't so bad. I take notice that the girl to guy ratio is about 1.25 to 1, and everyone appears to be making an attempt at being evenly spread out.

Suddenly, a guy wearing plaid shorts, a tight college shirt, and sunglasses, gets on a mic and welcomes us to college. He tells us to meet back here at the student union to be divided into subgroups where we will learn how to register for classes. He conveniently points me out from the crowd and asks Jesse and I to introduce ourselves. He's never seen someone wearing a tank top eat so much on the first night registration week. Jesse goes up there and gives a standard spill, "I'm Jesse. I'm from Memphis. I plan on studying Marketing and Brand Management."

(I take this opportunity to crack a joke. It isn't everyday someone hands you a microphone.)

"Hi, I'm Aaron. I'm a long-time listener, first time caller. I love long walks on the beach, candlelit dinners, and I own ten cats. I brought them here with me today, they are outside foraging for food at the moment. Naw, I'm just kidding. I'm also from Memphis and I plan on studying Health Sciences, possibly Chemistry or Biology."

The audience erupts in a slight laughter breaking the precedent and formal tone. I notice a table of girls beginning to whisper to one another and look my way. I stare back at them and they start to giggle indiscreetly at one of their friends. I hand back the mic to Plaid Shorts and return to my seat. After dinner, I head back to my dorm to get an early start to bed. When I make it there, I wonder if I made the right first impressions.

Chapter Twelve

Something's Missing

The schedule requests that students dress comfortably for the day. There are outdoor activities and team building exercises planned. Jesse and I make it to the student union and the crowd is larger than yesterday. There are tables set up with corresponding letters to divide us by our last names. In line, I stand behind one of the girls from the table last night that was giggling towards me. She has wavy brown hair, seems to be athletic, and is about my height. She's actually very pretty. She looks up at me and I take this opportunity to look at the messages from my phone. I pretend to not have been staring at her.

"Hey! You're Ten Cats guy, right?" the mystery woman asks.

"Oh yeah, that's me. I was just kidding, I don't really have 10 cats—more like 6. Four never came back from last night." I say with the straightest poker face.

She chuckles, "I know you aren't serious. My name is Vanessa by the way. You're Aaron from Memphis."

"Good to meet you Vanessa, are you from here?" I respond delighted that she remembers my name.

"I am originally from Arizona, I just came to this Tennessee College on a scholarship. So, I am a long way away from home." Vanessa says.

"Wow that's cool. Well I hope you enjoy it out here. I've lived in this state for well over fifteen years, so it is home for me now. What do you plan on studying?" I ask her.

"I want to do psychology or education, I have not decided quite yet." Vanessa responds.

While Vanessa and I talk more, I start to notice her accent is more formal than mine. I wonder if I sound weird to her. She seems to be a nice person. I know what it is like to be in a new place not knowing anyone—I just find ways to make people laugh to deal with the anxiety. I empathize with Vanessa and my southern hospitality keeps me cordial. Vanessa seems to have befriended me in the short while. We wait for our group leader to announce our next steps in the registration process.

"Which dorms are you in?" Vanessa asks me.

"Oh, I'm right by the Student Union. I am in Martin Hall on the first level. My best friend and I are roommates. I will have to introduce you guys sometime." I placate.

"Is your roommate the guy that spoke before you yesterday?" Vanessa recalls.

"Yep, that's him. He's hilarious, we never have a *dry* conversation or moment." I say with emphasis.

"Why the emphasis on the word *dry*?" She asks me with a peculiar look.

"Oh, he's just a standup guy. No reason." I say to recompose myself.

"Ha, you're funny. Give me your number so we can all meet up later then." Vanessa hands me her phone.

In the war of love, there are casualties and victims. I got caught slipping. Vanessa just ran game on me. Nah, no way. She's just being nice, I rationalize. But I like how smooth she was in getting my number. If she is not playing the field, I must be that charismatic. (Saying no would be rude.) Just as I am intimidated with having to make new friends, I'm sure she is the same way. Plus, I'm out of her league anyways. You only live once! We exchange numbers and then the group leaders begin shuffling us around to available computers to access the university portals.

The computer prompts me to enter in my credentials and assigns various options based on my interests. The first two years' worth of classes will be general courses and electives, spread out from 8am to 8pm offerings. Ouch! Long gone are the days of being done by 2pm on a Friday. I print out the options and take them to my guidance counselor who helps me walk through the best plan of attack for my college career. We meet at a side table where other students are paired alongside their counselors. My test scores recommended me for more advanced classes. The laziness in me just wants to be done as soon as possible. After a short deliberation of career goals, the counselor is anxious to help the next student. In less than 5 mins, a rough outline of my life is etched with graphite.

"Go sign up for these classes as soon as you can, otherwise you may not get a spot." The counselor recommends and sends me on my way.

I look up and see that Vanessa is already making new friends. I guess she is nice to everyone. Normally new girls avoid talking to me, but then again this is the first time I've not had Helen directly by my side. I feel my phone vibrate with an unexpected text.

"Where did you go? I just finished registration." Vanessa texts.

(I did not realize she and I moved up to the texting comfort level in the invisible arbitrary friend scale. Then again, friends do text one another. Why am I over analyzing this?)

"I am by the front door where we first met. What's up?" I respond.

"Help me get away from these losers!" She exclaims.

"Wait a minute, there's more than one of me here?" I joke back.

"No silly, you're cool. I'm by the middle row near the signs. Come quickly, please." She quickly replied.

I casually walk over there as if I hadn't located her before the text messages. Without hesitation, Vanessa runs to me and grabs my arm. The other guys take notice and begin to disperse one by one. They must assume I'm her boyfriend.

"Thank you so much! They wouldn't leave me alone. Sorry for grabbing your arm too hard. It was rude of me." Vanessa says.

I was blushing a bit as I told her not to worry about it. Although my first impression was an adlib about bringing ten cats to school with me; Vanessa seems to have bestowed her trust to me. We both laugh it off and sit together to review the schedule for the week. Based on our group numbers, Vanessa and I actually end up sharing the same itinerary. I feel awkward about disclosing to Vanessa that Helen and I are together. So, I do not. I rationalize that Vanessa has not asked me about anything romantic; therefore, I assume it would be rude to think that she must be attracted to me. The guys that were standing with her all looked better than me. Taller, more athletic, nicer clothes... why didn't she want their attention?

As we sit there together, I realize how close we physically are at the moment. She is less than two inches from the side of my hips. I have counted at least 5 jabs to my deltoid muscle while she laughed at my ridiculous jokes. By now, I am just saying whatever ridiculous statement I could think. Her smile is addicting to watch. For a moment, I catch a glimpse of her face up-close while she reads a text in her hand. Now I can observe in detail without looking like a creep. My heart begins to race as I memorize her unique features. Nothing seemed too exotic. Vanessa had dark brown hair, a slim face, beautiful blue eyes, and a sweet voice. She was somewhat like Helen in most ways; but something else about her intrigued me. It was the unknown that drew me to enjoy her company more. Even though Helen and I were back together; I still felt like something was missing, and meeting Vanessa revealed it.

Chapter Thirteen

In Too Deep

There was an event hosted by all the campus organizations, pretty much a picnic showcase of the interest groups around campus. Greek life, clubs, subject based committees, and various administration groups were handing out flyers with free food being offered. (I was going to go for the free food.) Jesse was more interested in the Greek life opportunities, he seemed to really want to branch out and make a name for himself. I went to the booths that offered samples of ribs and chicken. I saw a booth with a cat mascot and knew I needed to check it out.

"Here at the Chemists of American Technical Society (CATS) we believe that if you have mass and occupy space, then YOU matter!"

Oh no, not the puns. What am I getting myself into? These nerds were so corny, but I knew I needed to withhold my judgment. I came here to learn and the best way to learn is to step outside your box. Kirk and Mark are not here, so I have to make new friends. At least these people won't make fun of my massive forehead--half of them are already balding and they do not even look a day pass twenty. After signing up for the CATS club, I felt a familiar hand tap me on my shoulder.

I turned to see if it was Helen trying to surprise me on campus, it was actually Vanessa. She had brochures and goody bags in her hand from all the various tables. She had this smirk on her face.

"Did you just sign up for CATS? You really are crazy. Come on, let's go before you start meowing," Vanessa meows.

I follow her instinctively back to Martin Hall and help her with her bags. Instead of the usual left turn to the guy's side, she leads me to the right. Unsure if a guy can be wandering this side, Vanessa reassures me it's no big deal. Outside her door now, I see that she has decorated it with a whiteboard for messages, stickers of Arizona, and flowery stationary. The other doors are also decorated. The girls' wing puts the bland guys' side to shame. She invites me in and says she wants to relax for a second. For some reason, I felt like this was a bad idea. But I supposed since I made it this far, I should not limit my southern hospitality. I look around to make sure no one sees me enter, as if I need another reason to turn around at this instance.

I turn to close the door and when I turn to face the room, Vanessa is seated on her bed asking me to sit by her. I rest on the edge of the bed purposely, but she scoots closer. An audible gulp from my throat echoes through the room. She rests her head on my shoulders and tells me how happy she is to have met a regular guy. She tells me how all of the other people here are too talkative and don't seem interesting. (I hesitate to talk because I am unsure still of her motives, plus she cued me to shut up in so many words.) When she looks up at me, her eyes seduce me into a calmness.

"Before coming to Tennessee, my boyfriend broke up with me. He told me that he didn't want a long-distance relationship. I was running to get away from Arizona. Every guy up here has tried to talk to me, you're the only one that's made me laugh without reservations." Vanessa suddenly admits.

"Oh, I understand what you mean about being honest. For me, I just want to be real to myself. I'm sorry to hear that you're going through this at the moment. I cannot imagine how you feel," I lie.

"Don't worry about it. At the time, I thought I couldn't be without him; but now, I realize there's more to life than just him. I have my own future to worry about, plus there's plenty of things to keep my busy," She consoles to me.

"Yeah, same here. I just joined the CATS club, we both are about that life. The future holds limitless possibilities." I sarcastically mention.

She chuckles. Vanessa then looks at me and asks me, "What about you? Are you seeing anyone?"

"What do you want that answer to be? Would it make you think of me differently?" I question Vanessa, because I want to leave the opportunity for plausible deniability in the event this goes down as predicted.

"Just shut up. You boys talk too much" Vanessa whispers.

I do not even remember her leaning forward. The next thing I know, we are kissing. The euphoria of her lips sends an electrifying tingle to my skin and the hairs of my neck stand up. Her soft hands cup the edge of my chin and she pushes me back. Vanessa is surprisingly aggressive with her advances. I lose control of my balance and fall off the edge of the bed. You can hear a loud thump as I hit the ground.

"Oh my god! I am so sorry, I don't know what I was thinking. Are you okay?" Vanessa scrambles to say as I am laying on the floor.

"I'm fine, I'm fine. That was unexpected." I painfully jolt to stand back on my feet.

I probably deserved that rude awakening for this fantasy I'm perpetrating. I look at the phone in my pocket to see that Jesse is calling me. Using this opportunity to break the awkwardness, I answer.

"Yo, what's up, Jesse?" I say as I awkwardly avoid Vanessa's disappointed stare.

"Hey man, they are having an obstacle course tomorrow. I hear there will be a slip and slide. I've found my calling in life, bro!" Jesse says.

"Aww yeah, that's great. I'm busy at the moment, did you need something else or can I call you back? I am helping someone in their dorm move things," I confessed unsolicited.

"Naw that was it, just wanted to make sure you were alright. I am in the dorms and didn't see you here." Jesse remarks.

"I'll be back soon. We can go grab dinner and talk about our days later." I end the call.

"Bet" Jesse hangs up.

Vanessa is still red from the embarrassment of how I fell off the bed. I am still red from the clearly swollen elbow I used to cushion my fall. She tries to apologize to me again and mention how she does not normally kiss a guy so soon. This time I sit on the left side of her with the wall to my side. I stare at her for a moment and ignore the throbbing pain that is my arm. I wonder what I am getting myself into. A voice in my head is telling me to go for it. I wait for the other voice to counter that idea. I must have had a concussion, because I hear nothing. Either I must be speechless or it is due to the fact that Vanessa's lips have met mine once more.

Well damn, this is insane! I can taste the scent of her strawberry lips. Her unexplored body pressed on top of my square chested frame, while her long brown hair cascades against my ears. I can hear her inhale between our faces and exhale light puffs of air into my lungs. I am enthralled by her puckered lips, the softness of her skin etching the stubble of my face. By now she has mounted my hips and slips off her jacket. My hands are beside her waist. I contemplate how bad of a decision this is and how good she feels. I'm two seconds from telling her I cannot go through with this. She sees that I have a worried expression on my face. She takes off her jacket and covers my face with it to hide my worry. I remove it from my face to see that she was now shirtless and topless. The voice in my head is now silent. I am left with only two decisions now, "Which side of her am I going to start on first and where can I put my pants?" I am in too deep.

Chapter Fourteen

Thanks Bro

The next morning while brushing my teeth, I look at myself in the mirror. Vanessa left her marks on my neck. My arm is less red but still sore. It looks like I got into a fight with a vacuum cleaner and lost. I suppose I will be wearing a collar shirt today. I look through my closet and begin to pick out some clothes. Plaid shirt, khaki shorts, and tennis shoes will have to do today. The schedule mentions that we will be meeting fellow students and learning more about the school's history.

Jesse is wearing his usual get up and applies an extra dab of baby powder. We head out towards the quad in the center of campus. The gorgeous tall trees sprawl across the field; surrounding us are the colleges of various subjects. To the left is the engineering and sciences building. Humanities and mathematics encase the center of the expanse, with psychology and sociology in the far distance. The arts take over the north side besides the administration building. The bustling life of the campus comes alive with the university colors sprinkled on every yard of the sidewalk. This is college life! There is so much enthusiasm in the air, everyone seems to be excited for the first fun event.

I make a point to stick with Jesse today, I don't want to get myself in trouble again with Vanessa. I feel bad for cheating on Helen, I am going to do everything I can to make sure it does not happen again. There's no need to tell her, because it would only break her heart. I quickly text her sweet nothings while I have the time. They don't seem to erase the guilt that engulfs my mind.

"Morning love, can't wait to see you this weekend. Muah!" I cringe as I text. (Maybe that was a tad too obvious.)

"Me too! Love you!" Helen replies.

I feel relieved. Helen is not psychic. No one knows what happened except Vanessa. And even if Jesse did know, he wouldn't tell a soul. Hell, Jesse owes me for all the secrets I've kept for him.

Jesse and I once worked together at the movie theatres back in the day. We only took that job to be able to catch all the latest releases for free. We basically got paid to watch movies. We never did our jobs. One time, Jesse took a piss in one of the popcorn buckets left by the previous viewing. He told me to keep watch. Even though we didn't get caught, we still both lost our jobs. We didn't get fired. The movie theatre was shut down by health inspectors because they detected urine in the butter samples. There was a fall out of attendance which caused ticket sales to drop and eventually the movie theatre was shut down.

FRIENDS, LOVERS, OR NOTHING

Jesse and I walked up to some seats and listened to the announcer give us the directions. The obstacle course was to reinforce the concept of how college life will be overwhelming. Getting to the end will be difficult if you try to do it all alone. You have to learn to leverage your peers and the faculty to make things easier for you. It is a loop around the quadrangle and a scavenger hunt element is built into the course.

"On your mark, get set, GO!" The announcer yells on the bullhorn.

Thousands of students run towards their first challenge. For me, it is a makeshift ball pit. The objective is to cross the tight ropes. On one side are handles that say scholarships. People line up trying to cross the tight ropes on their own. One after one, people fall into the ball pit. They can continue the course but have to traverse a much longer distance. The balls slow them down. When it's time for Jesse and I to go, I suggest, "Let's use each other as support and walk the ropes together while we each grab onto the handles. As we step across, we realize this works surprisingly easier than what others attempted. But as we cross the midway point, one of Jesse's handles was rigged to fail. The imbalance causes both of us to fall. Fortunately, there was a path cleared for us already by those already in the ball pit. We race to the next challenge.

We are near the front as we approach a maze. Some people are blindly rushing through the maze without taking

74

time to consider what tools are around them to help. Jesse asks the coordinator if he can give us some tips. The coordinator says, "I breathe life giving air. But I cannot move."

"What is that supposed to mean? Are you deaf? That isn't what I asked. You got legs don't it? What do you mean you can't move?" Jesse begins to berate the coordinator. The coordinator just smiles and ignores Jesse.

"I think it's a clue, Jesse. I think he is referring to the trees. Let's climb that tree right there and see an aerial view of the maze before we enter." I conclude.

We go to the branch and mark out the flags above the maze. There are numbers 1-4. We can clearly see which directions will lead us astray. Up, down, left, right, and then straight are the directions we need to go to avoid the dead ends. It appears that the flags symbolize each year of college ahead of us. We easily move past this event and make it to the last leg of the race.

The final part is a gauntlet filled with gladiator like fights. Jesse and I suit up in protective gear and grab shields. People are allowed to enter in as pairs, but groups of 4 maximum at a time. People dressed in sumo wrestling costumes are there awaiting the groups. Each sumo wrestler has a unique word written on their headband. Partying, Drugs, Alcohol, Sex, Depression, Excuses, Fear, etc.… bounce us around the field. We individually cannot fight them off. We keep getting pushed back to the start of the line. Even though we have shields, they just expose us by our back side and spin us around.

"Let's all 4 of us link up and have each other's back. Use the shields to barricade up and use our increased mass to bounce them back."

The group agrees that it might just work. After we formulate the strategy, I take point in the front of the pack. Sure enough, the sumo wrestlers are unable to spin us around and we were able to charge to the end. We approach a giant slip and slide tarp in front of the finish. Jesse takes off his shirt and pants and screams, "I'm free!" Using Jesse as a boogie board, we skated our way over to be congratulated. Jesse's natural sweat mixed with the soap and water created an almost frictionless glide.

At the end, we receive a t-shirt welcoming us to college. They hand us a rolled-up sheet of paper fashioned like a diploma. Unraveled it reads, "Stick together, don't let Life stop you from reaching your goals." I look up and see that the other students behind us are all copying the same strategies. The obstacle course is quickly completed thereafter. I look at my clothes and body and see it covered in dirt and sweat. Thanks, Jesse

.

Chapter Fifteen

Stronger Than

Racing back to the dorms, Jesse and I fight to see who gets to take a shower first. Jesse ends up slipping in the middle of the hallway giving me the edge. I hurdle over his splayed body and run inside our dorm. Throwing aside my things, I am able to glance at my phone to see a few messages from Helen and Vanessa. Vanessa wants to know where my room is and what my plans are for the evening. Helen is bored and wants to chat. I tell Vanessa that I am in room 115 and am showering at the moment, and will hit her up later. I reply to Helen that I will call her after I finish my shower. The hot steam fills the bathroom and I wash off the salty brine that's covering my body. During the shower, I belch out a few of my favorite acapella jams enhanced by the echoed tiles. I sing and murder Prince's hit, "Do Me Baby". I embellish the last stanza just to annoy Jesse when I thought I heard him enter the room.

I come outside of the shower with a towel wrapped around my waist to see Jesse is shaking his head and smirking. I expected Jesse to be singing with me, but instead, he seems rather coy. I look to my left and realize that Vanessa was in our dorm, sitting on my side of the room, bursting out in laughter at the shock on my face.

"Do me baby? I never knew you could sing so well. What else are you hiding from me?" She opens after she is able to contain her laughs.

"Hi… Vanessa. I didn't know you was coming over right now. I see you have met Jesse. Jesse, why didn't you tell me we had company?" I ask Jesse.

"That's what you get for leaving me in the hallway you jerk!" Jesse boasts. (I guess I deserved that.)

Jesse then goes into the shower and gives Vanessa and me some privacy. I stand there trying to inconspicuously get dressed beside my closet.

"Are you pretending to be shy around me now? It's not like I have not seen it all before." Vanessa shouts.

"Keep it down! I don't want Jesse to hear you. Last time you got naked first, so this is entirely different. Let me just grab some pants real fast."

"Oh, so you are saying you don't want to be the only one naked in the room?" Vanessa wittingly concludes.

I slip on some long pants and turn around to see Vanessa has taken it upon herself to disrobe. I was not expecting this. She must think I'm a hoe or something. Dammit, why does she have to look so good? She locks the bathroom door to keep Jesse from being able to get back into the room. It was not necessary to lock the door, because Jesse's shower lasted way longer than I could. I told you, I was not a hoe. But I've only been here two days and already I've cheated on Helen twice. And it was even better the second time.

I finally manage to get dressed right before Jesse is beating on the door to get out of the bathroom. I open it and apologize that it was a slip of habit to lock the bathroom. Vanessa is clearly blushing, Jesse gives me the look of certainty. Jesse then grabs a few clothes and dresses himself in the restroom.

"So, what do we have planned tonight, you guys?" Jesse speaks from the bathroom.

"WE?!" I ask.

"Yeah, WE! You ain't leaving me here by myself like last night. You can't be the only roommate getting some now." He jokes unapologetically.

I turn to look at Vanessa and we shrug it off. There's no sense of hiding it now, especially since the cat is out the bag.

"Alright, Jesse. Let's hit the cafe up and get some lunch then. We need to go grocery shopping, too." I plan out loud.

We all walk together and exchange the normal pleasantries. Jesse seems to be genuinely impressed at my ability to randomly meet a girl on campus during the very first week. I am equally as impressed with myself. It's almost as if, the less you try, the more you get. At the cafe, we meet with a few of Vanessa's girlfriends that she knew from the obstacle course. They seem nice for the most part and don't seem to know anything about me. I breathe a sigh of relief, because I don't know how long I can keep this charade going between Vanessa and me. That's when I remembered that I never called Helen back.

I look at my phone and see that I have three missed calls and a text message all from Helen. I feel like a total jerk. I broke my word to Helen. I had no intention to not call her; but Vanessa was naked. I was naked, there was three minutes available, and I only needed two of those minutes, it would have been wrong to call Helen at that time anyways.

"You take the longest showers," Helen eye rolls me through her message.

"Sorry, out at lunch with Jesse. Will call you back tonight." I communicate.

I look up to see Vanessa staring at me like a piece of meat. What did I get myself into? Maybe it's the fact that I really don't want her attention that makes her want me so much. I make up my mind right then and there. I will not have sex with her again until I break up with Helen. It's not fair to either of us. How can I tell someone I love them and be unfaithful the very next day? Do I even want to be with Vanessa? So far, she's only shown me a physical attraction. There has to be more to her than just her looks.

After lunch, I recall that I still have not signed up for my classes. I tell Vanessa that I will talk to her later tonight at the coffee shop in the library. I run back to my dorm to complete my registration. While at my computer, I try to rationalize how I will inform Helen that we should break up. There really is no good reason in my head that I did not already debunk weeks ago when I couldn't stop thinking of Helen. Maybe I should just pretend Vanessa never happened. She's nice and all, but she clearly must be crazy to let me hit twice after meeting for only a day. Then again, what does that make of me?

Looking at the classes I opted to sign up for, there are only a few spots remaining. Unfortunately, they are either early morning classes, back to back, or late evening courses. Damn, I'm messing up my personal life being too consumed with these girls. Eh...it was worth it. I'm an early bird anyways and working late was a habit I picked up over the summer. I finally decide to call Helen to see how she is doing.

She picks up with the fondest voice I can hear. It feels like forever since we've talked. I don't really know where to begin. She asks me how were Jesse and I doing together as roommates and how was I adjusting to college. I tell her all about my first impressions of the campus and the various activities we've done so far--minus Vanessa of course. I think we spoke for at least 3 hours consecutively. I was foolish to ever betray her. She's at home waiting patiently for me, while

I am out gallivanting with some hoochie mama. A delightful, sweet, beautiful hoochie mama, but gallivanting nonetheless. Alright that's it. Vanessa has to go. I don't care how much she tries--I am stronger than this.

Chapter Sixteen

For Good Measure

It's been two days since I've spoken to Helen. I wake up beside Vanessa to her wild hair covering my face. It's Friday and I know this is the weekend I said I would come home to visit before life gets too hectic. Who would have known I would have been creating my own hell? I don't even remember the excuse I last gave Helen for why I haven't called. I slide out of bed being sure not to disturb Vanessa. She seems not to even notice me leave the room.

Back in my dorm, I prepare my bag for the weekend. I make sure to bring home the college apparel for my parents. They requested t-shirts and hats to boast to their friends. By now, Vanessa has woken up and texted me that she'll miss me and wishes she could come, too. I told her it would be way too soon to be bringing home a new girl from college and that we should take things slow. Plus, my parents don't know I am coming home to break up with Helen. I really don't want to break things off with Helen, but I know it's the right thing to do. I understand why she wanted to be just friends earlier this summer--if I had dealt with it alone, I would not have all this guilt.

FRIENDS, LOVERS, OR NOTHING

I realize also that I have not even told Vanessa about Helen. We have already gone past the point of no return, there's no need in me being honest now. My chest is heavy with the pending conversation on my mind. Helen deserves better. I was able to find someone new in less than a week of being apart. Helen deserves someone who is not as weak of a person as I am that would cheat. I am not going to tell Helen my reason, I want to just tell Helen she and I need to take a break. College is overwhelming and I feel bad not being able to text and talk to her as often as I'd like. She may not accept my response, but it's better than the truth. The truth that I am sleeping with a girl I barely know and I don't intend to stop. I wouldn't even consider Vanessa a girlfriend. She's just convenient and I never realized how much work I was putting in to keeping myself happy with Helen. Vanessa just wants to enjoy my company, there's no bad history, no commitments, and it's something different.

The short drive home felt like forever. I knew better than to turn on the radio in my car to avoid having to listen to the universe dictate my emotions. I made up my mind while driving in silence past the farms and small towns. I make it home just before noon and notice that Helen is parking in front of my house. We walk inside and my parents are pretty ecstatic to see me. It's only been 5 days, but it feels like it's been longer. I went from having their guidance and support every day to being on my own with absolute freedom. It has really changed my perspective. I give them the college swag in my bag and they proceed to ignore me for the rest of the afternoon. I walk up to Helen and give her a hug. She squeezes me tightly and kisses me without a second of hesitation. The old me resurfaces and I feel numb with emotions of love. I lose all confidence in myself that letting Helen down easy, would be easy. She's just as beautiful as I remember and I forget about the week-long escapade between Vanessa and me.

Helen and I walk up to my room and sit on my bed to talk. The room feels vacant without my clothes in the closet and being unoccupied for the week. Helen kisses me again and I begin our conversation with the first words to come to mind.

"Hi Helen, I've missed you."

"I've missed you, too, Aaron."

"I got you a jacket, hopefully it isn't too big." I say after displaying her the gift.

"I don't want a new jacket. You wear it first and then give it back to me later so I can remember you when I wear it." Helen tells me after she tries it on.

"Are you always going to be this busy with school? We hardly spoke these last few days. I began to worry and couldn't wait for today to come." Helen reports to me.

"Sorry, love, I was just preoccupied with trying to get established on campus and running several errands before the weekend. I didn't expect college to take such a toll on my social life," I carefully explain.

An awkward silence fills the room. Helen seems to be okay with my explanation. She turns away to collect her thoughts for a moment. After that moment, I see a worrisome look in her eyes.

"I know this may seem like a repeat what I am about to say Aaron, but maybe we should take a break then… I don't want you to get distracted and I had plenty of time apart to realize that we are perfectly capable of being apart. I have been preoccupied with work anyways." Helen says without shedding a tear.

I sit there for a second for a purposeful dramatic pause. I am relieved to know that I didn't have to open the conversation for us to break up. We come to an agreement that things will be better this way. I know I should tell her about Vanessa, but the means would not change the outcome. There is not much solace this time around. Helen and I are able to comprehend what life will be like now after a 1-week trial. I used to feel numb and senseless when we broke up before. But now I just feel a warmth of freedom. Or maybe this is what it is like when my guilty sensations evaporate from my consciousness. We do not exchange many more words; enough has been said about the subject. She stares at me then presses her lips against mine for what seems to be an eternity. Everything about Helen is still there for me to love. I doubt that I am everything that she still remembers. I hold her hand in mine and lace our fingers together. I tell her, "I love you," just for good measure before she leaves.

Chapter Seventeen

Slow Down

Sometimes, I cannot keep wishing for things to change in life. I have to fight for what I want. People will get hurt, it's inevitable. So, if I can prevent someone from getting hurt, while still getting what I want, I should. This will balance out the wrongs that I have done. The right thing for me to do is to make sure that I am not making a mistake. If Helen and I are meant to be, there's nothing I can do to change that outcome. If Helen and I are not meant to be, then at least I know she found happiness somewhere outside of us. No, I'm not trying to rationalize cheating, I just believe that the end goal for any relationship is happiness. If Helen is happy, then that's all that matters...right? She will be happier not knowing. Either way, the result is the same. We aren't together.

The drive back to campus seems shorter than the first time around. Maybe it's because I spend less time staring out the side windows and focused on the road ahead. When I get back to my dorm, all I want to do is surround myself with new faces. I can actually focus on getting to know Vanessa without having to hold back. I feel tired being held to some antiquated standard I set during high school. I have to change how I approach life, because college is not high school. But now that Helen's standard for me has been redacted, I can be myself. Whoever that may be. The only person that knows me up here is Jesse. Everyone else, I'm meeting for the first time. I cannot let this opportunity to venture out in the world pass me by. It's normal to want something different. This must be why I am so drawn to Vanessa, I feel like every time she laughs at one of my recycled jokes there is a newness of emotions that overcomes me. Who would have known three months ago where'd I'd be today?

I look down and notice that my gas tank is approaching empty. I stop in a small town an hour outside of campus. The sign reads, "Welcome to Bluefield". How ironic that I find myself stopping in a field of blueness. There's nothing for me to feel blue about, I actually am somewhat racing back to meet Vanessa. I walk into the fuel station to deposit twenty dollars for the pump. The clerk was heavily entrenched in a crossword puzzle located in this morning's paper.

I cough to clear my throat, "Excuse me, the word you are looking for '47 Across' is MOLASSES."

The clerk surprisingly agrees and writes it in his puzzle before starting my transaction.

"Where you from young man?"

"Oh, I'm from Memphis. On my way up for school." I respond.

"Oh, that's great. I did not know Egyptians could speak English so goods," the clerk says without hesitation.

"No sir, I am Asian."

"I know that, but you are from Memphis--so you are an Asian Egyptian. I hope you learn something while you are up there in school."

I bid the clerk farewell and hurriedly speed off to make up for the lost time during the pit stop. Before I could even make it over the top of the town's ridgetop, flashing blue lights approach my rear bumper. I pull to the side and park ten feet in front of a 45mph-speed limit sign. The officer walks over to my passenger side window and asks me to roll it down.

"Evening officer, to what do I owe the pleasure for this stop?"

"You know you were speeding 44 mph in a thirty-five, don't you?"

"Umm… this sign says, 45."

"Yeah it does, but you haven't made in front of it yet. Back there it says 35."

I basically got caught in a speed trap and didn't realize it. I was so anxious to leave the gas station, I made a careless mistake. Now I'm wondering if I can talk my way out of it. It's too late to put on a foreign accent. He asks for my license and registration and returns to his cruiser. After fifteen minutes or so he returns to my passenger window. My hazard lights are reflecting off his badge and belt buckle.

"Since you are in a rush, I want to hear where you are headed before I make a decision on whether or not to write you a ticket. You aren't from around here and you have no warrants. Maybe this will teach you to slow down in the future. What's so important that you can't observe the laws around you? You are too young, your parents would not want you to be this irresponsible. You got your whole life ahead of you son."

I have no idea why this trooper is lecturing a stranger, but I appreciate being able to have the chance to be let off with a warning. Do I tell this cop I am racing to see a girl at school? Maybe, I should give him the whole country song alibi--my girl left me, I ran out of gas, and my parents kicked me out the house.

"Sorry Officer, I must have had too much on my mind, I did not notice the speed changed back there."

"Well what's on your mind, kid?"

"I'm starting school next week and I was late to see a lady friend of mine. I did not want to keep her waiting."

"That's obviously sweet of you, but is she worth getting a ticket or worse, driving off a cliff because you were in a rush?"

"I wouldn't say anyone is worth that, sir."

"Well if you know that, you should slow down. You see that you ended up losing time and not gaining time when you are in a rush, big fella."

"Does this mean I am not getting a ticket?"

"I didn't say all that. We aren't done talking... Mr. Aaron Pp..Platypus"

"It's pronounced Plattenburg"

"I don't care what you are eating for dinner, son. Just drive safely and get out of here. You're ID is clear. Now clear your mind as well."

By now, I have had enough of this Bluefield town. I carefully wait to make sure the officer's lights are faintly in the distance before I speed back up and enter my college town. Vanessa is there to greet me by the entrance near my side of the building. She is motioning her hands to tell me to hurry up. She looks at me as if it's been an eternity. I kiss her under the arch of the doorway and hold the door from her. I stare into her eyes and can tell that she's missed me. Yet for some reason, I can't help but think of the officer's words. I feel like I'm moving too fast. This is first time I've taken the time to look at Vanessa genuinely, guiltless. I have been living in a bustling city too long. Maybe this small town is starting to grow on me or maybe for once I'm just starting to slow down.

Chapter Eighteen

She Gets Me

I made a point today to not be late. A subtle change to what I normally do. First impressions on my first day of college means something, right? I'm taking Calculus I at eight in the morning, four days a week. I figure math is easiest in the morning so you have the rest of the day to think about it. I was sadly mistaken when I met the professor. When I sat down in the front row, I noticed that the fellow students meandered closer to the back until all the seats beside those in the front were filled. The professor came in the class wearing tight dark khakis, pocket protectors, and a short sleeve pinstripe shirt. When he wrote on the board "Dr. Dallas", he made sure to drag the "S" to underline his whole name. He grabbed a large textbook out of his bag and dropped it flat on the wooden desk. The sound ended all the chatter within the room.

"Today Class, is the first day of the rest of your lives. For some of you it's the 2nd first day of the rest of your lives because you failed me last year. I'm looking at you in the back. I hope you all realize that if you sat in the front maybe you'd learn a thing or two. Did you all know that 95% of all students will earn better grades if they had just sat in the T-zone of the class? Look at these fresh faces, sitting in the T-zone. What's your name, sir?"

"Who me? I'm Aaron Plattenburg. Does this mean I am getting an automatic 95 for my grade in calculus?"

"Very funny. No. It just means you have a 95% chance to not be in the 5% of those that still manage to fail while being in the T-Zone."

"Challenge accepted," I replied. The class erupts in a giggle of laughter.

"What does that even mean?" Dr. Dallas replies with a bewildered look.

"A man never reveals his secrets on the first date, Dr. Dallas." By now I've set the impression that I will say whatever, whenever there is an audience. And I am probably going to fail this course now.

I look to my left and a new face is blushing from holding in her laughter. Either she's laughing with me or at me. She has a natural look to her round face. A face that's now covered after she notices I hear her giggles. She turns her face back to her textbook and pretends the table of contents called her attention.

"Mr. Platypus, you and I are going to be the best of friends-- we shall see if you can manage to keep that attitude for 15 weeks. Class, open your textbooks to Chapter 1 'Integrating Functions'," the professor quickly resets to his agenda.

I whisper to my left, "Well clearly you know my name, what's yours?"

"I'm Michelle, you shouldn't be talking during class," she turns away and intently faces forward.

You can't win them all, I guess.

That hour I learned that Isaac Newton invented calculus in the 17th century. During that time, mathematics did not have the capacity to solve the complexities of gravity, physics, and astronomy. Newton's success was not appreciated by all, there was another great mind, Leibniz, who claimed Newton plagiarized his work. The two could never come to an agreement. This then made me realize that someone may have cheated and the truth would never be known. I took solace in this because it rationalized how I cheated on Helen. I start thinking about the past again in a daze only to be disrupted by Dr. Dallas.

"Mr. Platypus, I repeat, what are your thoughts on what is the derivative of the number '21'?

I was not paying a lick of attention. Think, think, think, Aaron! Twenty-one divided by 3, minus the 4, equals 3, three is the number of times I watched the Titanic that one weekend with Helen, oh crap…

"Zero." I blurt. Because that's what I feel like at this moment.

Dr. Dallas reluctantly admits I was right and proceeds to write more gibberish on the whiteboard. At this point,

Michelle stares at me blankly, astonished. I must have changed my impression on her.

"That was a lucky guess!" She whispers.

"You should be paying attention you know," I wink.

Michelle's face is red with embarrassment. The clock reads 9 o'clock and the sound of closing books means it is time to leave. Before I can continue my conversation with Michelle, she scurries out into the hall and I lose her in the crowd. She's both short and nimble or she was just a figment of my vivid imagination.

I check my phone and see that Vanessa has been texting me during class.

"Why did you sign up for a morning class? You woke me up when you left the bed. Uhh…" Timestamped 8:15 am

"Earth to Aaron babe, you hear me talking to you. Don't be a nerd and learn too much. Your forehead is already big enough. Xoxo" Timestamped 8:40 am

"Breakfast in the student union?" Timestamped 9:01am

I respond, "Sure. I'll be there in 5 minutes. And of course, I am a nerd. I get it from you."

I walk through the Humanities halls to catch the elevator. I see Ellis, he holds the lift open for me. Ellis remembers me from ROAR week.

"TEN CATS! Good seeing you again brother. Where you headed?"

"I'm about to meet up with someone for breakfast. Just got out of Calculus, I need to replenish with some brain food. I have not eaten a thing since yesterday."

"Cool, you mind if I join you? I was headed that way myself. These buffets are the best."

"Sure, the more the merrier. Us freshmen got to stick together, especially Memphis folk."

We arrive to the café to see a long line has formed by the front to swipe our identification cards. Vanessa is almost at the front and tells me to cut ahead. I scurry in shame, but oblige. Ellis tags along. The students behind us don't seem to care as they stare face deep into their infinite scrolling phones. Vanessa lands a kiss on me as soon as I get beside her in line.

"This your girlfriend, Aaron? I didn't mean to interrupt your breakfast. I just thought you were eating with some friends" Ellis politely asks.

By now, Vanessa is awaiting my response. I have no guilt about it, but she and I never discussed what we were so I default to cracking a witty response.

"I mean, I just needed some quick CPR from a complete stranger." I respond.

Vanessa seems to be happy enough with my response. I escape with plausible deniability mentally, but physically, Vanessa laces her dainty fingers across my palm. She squeezes my hand and says, "Don't worry we can share him this one time for breakfast. But later he's mine."

Ellis laughs and we all proceed to have our first breakfast as official college students.

Chapter Nineteen

So Unexpected

Almost a month has passed since classes have begun.   The days seem to grow shorter and shorter. Helen and I text but it's just cordial memos, she seems to miss me. I do not ignore any of her messages, I just make sure not to commit to anything besides small talk. She seems to be enjoying her job and has not had much time to play phone tag with me anyways.

Vanessa is still warming up to her classes and feels that psychology is probably going to be her major. I'm not surprised since her mind games and body drive me crazy. The other night, she asked me what did I want for dinner. She suggested we go out and get some Italian food. After I deliberated with her for 10 minutes on other options, I was able to make the choice that Italian food was the best option. She proved that it was in my best interest. We came to a compromise. She said we can take dessert home, if we go to an Italian restaurant. Vanessa called her deal the "Caramel Tira Mi-Sutra". Who am I to say no?

During dinner, we notice that the venue is moderately packed. You can see the blend of clientele stretch from bar singles, to older couples, to college student groups, and young couples.

"So why am I so lucky to have kept your attention this long?" I ask Vanessa.

"What do you mean? You're you. I feel like I am lucky to have you in a world full of strangers."

"I could have been crazy, you didn't have to befriend me so quickly. How did you know I wasn't crazy?"

"I figured most crazy people do not admit they are crazy. You admitted to having ten cats and you're too cute, so I took a chance."

"Now you are just trying to run up the bill. I'm glad to have met you. There is something special about you. I wonder sometimes if you like me as much as you say you do."

Vanessa is about to respond, but then the host calls us up to show us our table. I watch Vanessa's face as her patience is rewarded. She has this smile on her face that is additive. She seems to be delighted and very happy. We are seated near the back of the restaurant in a booth. We both sit on the same side together. They remove the wine glasses without hesitation and present us the dinner menu. Tonight's special is mushroom ravioli in a truffle alfredo sauce paired with an appetizer of lasagna fritters.

I order the special, Vanessa came for the breadsticks and soup. I don't mind because it's a very affordable meal for a college budget. She's not too proud to ask for more free bread either after she devours the first tray.

"So, you had me take you to this nice restaurant just for bread?" I ask her.

"I love their bread. Don't sass me! You had plenty of other options to choose before you decided to take me here." Vanessa blames.

"Touché"

Her humor complements me so well. I feel like we compete to annoy one another. We usually settle it by me gracefully conceding. As she slurps her soup, I stare at how beautiful she is. Her hair is tied back in a simple bun, haphazardly placed in no particular fashion. She's wearing my sweat pants paired with a college hoodie. My clothes look better on her than me. Vanessa does not even have to try and impress anyone. Even at this moment she leaves me breathless. The way she cradles her spoon gently to her bowl, blows a sweet kiss over the tiny ladle until cool, and opens her mouth to eat. I'm watching her in slow motion, growing ever more infatuated. The pleasure she feels when she pairs the soup with each bite of garlic bread. "This is so good!" She tells me without offering me a taste. By now she's brought her feet off the floor into the booth and sits with her calves crossed. She's in her own little heaven as well. She seems to be so care-free. My daze is interrupted once my food arrives.

"Would you like cheese on your meal, sir?" The waiter asks me.

"Sure, not too much, I am cheesy enough."

"With that joke, I am not one to disagree." The waiter says.

Vanessa laughs and calls me a goof.

"Would you two like more bread?"

"Yes, please. Could we have an extra bag of bread to-go as well?"

The waiter gives us a wink of assurance. Vanessa thinks I am a hero. If she wasn't too busy with a mouth full of bread, I am sure she would tell me thank you. I start to eat my food before it gets cold. The mushroom ravioli was a good choice. I normally prefer fast food but this is something I can grow accustomed. The sauce is a thick broth of parmesan with a hint of oregano. The ravioli pasta is tender and perfectly paired with an appropriate portion of ground mushrooms. Vanessa steals the last few bites from my plate.

"See, I don't need to order my own dish. I can just eat from your plate," She quirks.

"You're right, I could stand to lose some weight. This is a good symbiotic relationship."

"Relationship? So, you dropped the R-word finally. Do you like being in a *relationship*, sir Aaron?" She facetiously asks.

"Oh lord, I am clearly too involved in my biology classes. I am already talking too much science. I regret saying anything now."

"Don't worry, my sweet nerd. I like this relationship as much as you do. But it could be better."

(What could possibly be better than what we got for now? I should have never even said anything.)

"Is it my forehead? I don't think there's any cosmetic craniotomies that can fix what I got going on. What more do you want from me, woman?" I ask confusingly.

"You are so silly. Your forehead is only moderately huge. I was just implying that it would be better if we can have dessert."

I grab the menu and review the options for her. "They got some gelato, chocolate mousse, and tiramisu." Vanessa places her hand over my inner thigh. (Oh, this is what she means by dessert.)

I grab the waiter's attention, "Check, Please! And don't forget the bread."

On the drive back to campus, Vanessa stashes the leftovers on the floor of the passenger side. As she takes her time to buckle her seat, I ponder if my heart is thinking clearly. Why do I feel that a part of me has grown attached to her? Is it simply due to a lack of blood in my brain at the moment? She is an amazing person and great company, but it all feels too good to be true. We arrive back at Vanessa's empty dorm. Her roommate conveniently left for the weekend. Vanessa departs momentarily to change into something more comfortable. I can hear her brushing her teeth shortly after, humming a tune in the bathroom.

I get a text message from Helen. "Are you busy?"

"Not yet. What's up?"

"I know you are probably getting ready for bed, and I wouldn't bother you unless it was important. Can I call you?"

"Sure, give me a second. I will call you." I text.

Vanessa comes out from the restroom wearing a pink satin nightgown. The material barely covers the top of her ass which is draped in a nearly transparent sequin with white lacing. The miniature bows accent the center of her voluptuous chest and the center of her navel. Vanessa grabs my phone out of my hand and kisses my whole mouth with hers. She traces my entire inner jaw with her tongue. I am overwhelmed by the taste of her lips, it is very minty. I could have not expected a better end to the evening. We explore each other's bodies for what it seems to be an eternity. When we are done, I glance up at my phone to see only twenty minutes have elapsed. Vanessa appears content. She smushes my cheeks with her hand as she props herself up to walk over to the bathroom. I reach for my phone to silence its buzzing. Helen is still texting me.

"Are you going to call soon? It's okay if you can't talk right now. But I just wanted you to know that I may be pregnant."

Chapter Twenty

Sure Thing

I'm staring at my phone in silence. Rereading Helen's text over and over wondering if my phone has the wrong number saved. What the hell am I going to do? I thought teen pregnancies end after you leave high school. This is what happens when you let the basketball coach teach sex education. We spent 2 hours watching a documentary about nature and statistics—in the end I learned that the mitochondria are the powerhouse of the cell.

Vanessa comes back to bed wearing the sweat pants from dinner and one of my t-shirts. I rest the phone face down on my chest and avoid eye contact with her.

"Wow, I've never left you speechless before. Must have been nice," She says.

"It was incredible. I enjoyed dessert very much. I just want to take in this moment because it's not often I have nights end like this." I deflect to her. "Wait here, I need to go back to my room and grab a change of clothes."

"Take as long as you need, I got what I wanted already," Vanessa reveals as she cuts on her tablet beside the bag of garlic bread.

I walk into my dorm to see that Jesse is playing video games in his underwear with the AC on. He doesn't even notice me with his headset over his ears. I can definitely hear him screaming at his online teammate though.

"What the fuck! Shoot him! He's right there. What do you mean where? Right THERE! Oh my god!" Jesse yells before throwing his controller across the room.

"Oh, Hey Aaron, I thought you were with Vanessa for the night. Do you want me to put pants back on?"

"No, you're okay. I just needed to make a call really fast."

"Good because I wasn't going to put any pants back on even if you said so." Jesse then gets up to go to the restroom to take an abnormally long piss.

I lay down on my bed and dial Helen's number. It rings a few times before I hear her voice. She seems to have been waiting up for me to call. It sounds like she is wiping her eyes before saying hello.

"Hi Helen, I got your message. What's going on?"

"Thanks for calling. It's been a crazy couple of days this week. I'm late and I am freaking out. I didn't know who else to call. I haven't even told my parents. I'm really nervous."

"Calm down, everything will be alright. We are going to do what we got to do, just take a deep breath. Babies don't come overnight so we have plenty of time to plan."

107

"Aaron, I appreciate you stepping up but I have to be honest with you. If I am pregnant, I'm not 100% positive that it would be yours."

"What? What do you mean?"

"I'm seeing someone, well kind of. But there's no way I can tell that person about this right now. I just wanted to talk to you because I feel so alone right now. I can't really trust anyone, not even myself—I was always so careful with us."

"I don't know what to say. I'm surprised to hear that you are already seeing someone. Does that mean you were being reckless with some dude?"

"I'm always careful! This isn't just about you, Aaron. I thought you would understand and want to know. Forget I even said anything."

"So, you are going to hang up on me as quickly as you drop this bomb on me?"

"No Aaron, I can't focus on me and my life if you just expect to have things your way. You're the one that left for college and chose not to stay closer. I'm the one that's always waiting for you to text me. You never seem to even care about what's going on in my life. I figured you'd care to know that you may be a father soon."

"I'm sorry, look I am not trying to argue. I just don't know either. I mean, this is a lot to take in. I need some time to think. Please don't resent me for it."

"Okay, fine. Thanks for calling me back. We can talk more tomorrow. When will you be back in town?"

"Maybe by Labor Day or Fall Break. I don't know. It depends on my class schedule and workload. I'm enjoying it up here, but I want to be there for you if you need me. I just can't promise you anything right now. I have to go. I'll call tomorrow in the evening. Goodnight Helen."

As I rummage through my desk to put my books into my backpack, I notice the tin of love letters Helen returned. I open them, finding myself staring at Helen's photo from when we went to the park together that day. It was senior skip day. The whole gang was there. Helen has her face turned towards me as I am smiling for what appears to be in the middle of a laugh. On the back of the photo she writes her name as Helen Plattenburg. I used to think we were soulmates. I am angry now with jealousy to think she's moved on so quickly. Although I've already moved on myself, I always expected a way back to her. I can't waste anymore emotions or time tonight. I push the tin aside on my desk and prepare to leave my dorm room again.

"Yo Jesse, can I talk to you about something serious?"

"Look, it's a serious condition. It's called Hyperhidrosis. It's natural. I'm wet, it's just sweat!"

"No not that. Helen called to tell me she may be pregnant and that it probably could be mine."

"You dirty dog you! Wait, what do you mean probably?"

"Apparently she's been seeing someone else."

"Yikes. That's crazy because you just started seeing Vanessa, too. Does she know about Helen?"

"No, I just found out. You're the only other person that knows. Should I be worried?"

"I mean, when was the last time you guys did the do?

"I think it was maybe 4 or 5 weeks ago, before we drove up to school. I'm pretty sure I was careful."

"Well, how long has she been seeing this other dude?"

"I don't know. But if she's late, then it can't be much longer than 5 weeks or shorter than 3 weeks I would guess."

"How do you know she wasn't talking to him longer than that? Did she mention how far along the pregnancy is?"

(That's when it dawned on me. Maybe Helen, too, was unfaithful. Events are starting to formulate in my mind.)

"You're right. I don't know. I didn't even think to ask. I will ask her tomorrow. Hell, she doesn't know about Vanessa. Vanessa doesn't even know about Helen."

"Yeah, welp. That sucks. I would give you a hug right now but I'm sure you'd prefer I don't."

"Thanks anyways, man. I'll be back tomorrow morning. I'm going to spend the evening at Vanessa's tonight."

"Make sure you pull out this time when you finish. Ha. Sorry, I had to say it. At least we know that your mitochondria work and you aren't sterile. I'm wishing the best for you either way."

I leave for the door and lock it behind me. Phone in hand, Vanessa is wondering if I got lost. I scurry along and sneak down the hallway to not bring any attention to myself. In a few minutes I am at her door. I stand a foot in front of it and hover my knuckles in the air. I'm hesitant to knock because I want to gather my composure. But one question still seems to linger on my mind. Was Helen faithful to me before we broke up? Because I know for sure I pulled out!

Chapter Twenty-One

Fistful of Regrets

The weekend is finally here and all I want to do is pretend last night's conversation with Helen wasn't real. The morning sun is reflecting throughout the room, lighting up every corner of the room. I can hear Vanessa is overly excited while putting on her running shoes. Apparently, I should have told her to stop at one bag of bread and now I have to help her lose the 2 pounds she gained from yesterday. Cutely, everything seems to be my fault with her. I must be a glutton for punishment. Vanessa regrets eating so many carbs and wants to burn off the damage.

"I don't have any running clothes so we need to head back to my dorm, you can go without me—I don't want to keep you waiting." I contest to her.

"Well we better hurry up. I can feel my neck doubling in size. I don't mind waiting a few extra minutes." She says.

I'm too tired to argue, so we gallop over to my room. We enter and see that Jesse is still sleeping. I quietly get dressed in front of my closet. Vanessa impatiently takes a seat by my desk. I can hear her sighs hurrying me.

As I locate my shorts and long sleeve sweat proof shirt, I hear the sound of the metal tin container being open. Vanessa's tapping foot seems to have found its footing entrenched in my past love letters.

"What is this Aaron? Who is this?" Vanessa confronts me.

"This is nothing. She's my ex-girlfriend. Why are you going through my things?" I frustratingly ask.

"Ex? Why do you keep a box of letters from your ex? Why is it out on your desk?"

"This is really none of your business. I thought you wanted to go run. Let's go!" I dismiss.

I grab the tin and close it. Putting it back into my desk. Our voices disturb Jesse and he wakes up.

"Hey, if y'all gone be loud at least wait until I've taken a piss. Have some respect!"

"Sorry Jesse, we are about to leave in a second."

We head out and down the hall, not before Vanessa stares at me with a sorrowful look. Her silence resonates. She is keeping an active two steps in front of me. I pace myself to keep up, but the challenge increases with each stride.

Once outside, Vanessa asks me again, "Who is she?"

"Her name is Helen, if you must know. We went to high school together, she still lives back home in Memphis. We are not together."

"Why do I get the feeling there's more to her than just that. I've never kept any of my ex boyfriend's love letters."

"Why did you go through my things? This isn't about you. I accidentally packed them in my things. She gave them back to me, and I never threw them away. It's not a big deal. Not everyone does things the way you handle things. If it makes you feel better, I'll get rid of them."

"How long were you together?" Vanessa returns back.

"Look, I can run or I can talk… I can't do both." I protest to her.

"Fine." She ends.

We jog to about the other side of campus in silence. My lack of exercise begins to take notice. Those damn raviolis got me feeling like a marshmallow in a microwave. Vanessa is running with a head full of steam. I'm starting to catch a cramp.

"Wait, wait, hold on… I need to take a break." I pant.

"You okay?" She finally says words to me.

"Yeah, just catching a cramp. I don't think I fully digested everything from last night." I nearly barf out.

"Alright, since you aren't running anymore... you can talk now."

(How do I fake a concussion from dehydration?)

"What do you want to know?"

"Do you still have feelings for your ex?"

"That's irrelevant. I have emotions for everyone but I have my own preference and decisions."

"Sounds like that's a yes. How long did you guys date?"

"Couple years. Off and on."

"Why did you break up?"

"I moved to college and met you."

Vanessa's angry tone seems to disappear in her silence.

"What do you mean when you met me?"

"She broke up with me before I came to school. We tried to work things out. But once I met you, I realized that I wasn't committed to making it work." I try to explain carefully.

"Was this before or after we slept together?"

"I wanted to tell you, but I just wasn't expecting that night to happen. I never for a second thought you were interested in me. I really was just being nice, and one thing led to another so quickly. I never intended to leave Helen until I realized you existed."

"Aaron, I left my past in Arizona. My ex cheated on me. I've had my heart broken enough times to know that I needed to get away from that idiot. I can't believe I am a part of helping you cheat. I really thought you were different from other guys Aaron."

"What are you saying? Are you trying to end things between us because you forgot to ask me if I was single? How am I supposed to know what's on your mind before you share it? I did the right thing and broke up with Helen. She and I are still friends, things are fine between us. Why are you tripping?"

"Does she know about me?"

"Why does that even matter?"

"So, there's your answer. She's only still friends with you because she doesn't know about me. I want to talk to her."

(Oh, hell naw. Vanessa must be out her damn mind to be trying to link up with my future baby mama. I've seen plenty of day time talk shows to know how this ends up. The crowd will not be chanting my name in that episode.)

"No, I am not comfortable with that. You can't go through my things and expect me to let you go through my past as well. That's like me asking if I can be homies with your ex-boyfriend."

"You can be, because if not, I don't think we can be together. I don't really trust you right now. If you were willing to lie to your girlfriend about me, cheat on her with me--I can only imagine what you are hiding from me."

(She puts Freud to shame... Damn she's good.)

Somehow, the gods have lifted my spirits and the cramps are magically dissipating. I get up and take a deep breath. Vanessa is demanding a response. I look deep into her eyes and kiss her. She pushes me back gently. Before she can open her eyes, I am in my 2nd gear stride, sprinting back to my dorms.

"Aaron, where the hell are you going? Don't you run away from me!" Vanessa screams.

I can hear her trailing me by about 20 yards now. She's running full speed. Over the hill I can see the top of our dorms. I just got to make it back before she does.

"Just wait until I catch up, I'm going to beat your ass, Aaron!"

"You got to catch up first, slowpoke." I mock.

I make it into the lobby about 10 steps ahead and cut left to the men's side. I slide into home base with my key in hand to unlock the door. I drop the key. Vanessa has turned the corner at the end of the hall. She sees me. I pick up the key and finally make my way inside.

I grab the tin box and hide it on Jesse's side of the room behind his stash of baking soda. I run into the bathroom and sit on the toilet. Vanessa opens the door to the dorm.

"Why did you run away?"

"Because I don't want to talk about it."

"So, are you going to let me talk to her or what?"

"You really want to have this conversation right now?"

"I just want to know who I am up against. Clearly she means something to you for you to behave this way."

"Look, Helen is seeing someone else. It doesn't matter."

"Quit saying it doesn't matter. It matters to me. I am not going to let my heart be broken twice because you can't admit your feelings about Helen. You can't even admit your feelings about me. I'm not to be toyed."

"Well quit playing games then! You can't just set the rules for what you want then get mad at the outcome not in your favor. I deserve my privacy to my past and to my bathroom breaks. I don't know what you want from me." Aaron yells.

"I don't know what I want from you. But this is not something I want for myself." Vanessa confirms.

Vanessa slams the door. Jesse is laughing in the background.

"Bro, are you in there shitting? Because I need to go myself and I am not too ashamed to use the shower." Jesse asks me.

"Nah, not really. I just wanted her to leave."

"Well get out of there. Don't bring them crazy ass girls in our room. This is my domain, too. Get your stuff out of my drawer. These letters don't have enough absorption for my needs."

I come out from hiding in the bathroom. Jesse hands me the tin box. I can feel my hands fill with regret.

Chapter Twenty-Two

Unfamiliar

It's nearing four o'clock and Vanessa has ignored every last one of my text messages. She must be still pissed at me. I could use some time to think anyways. God, I'm such an idiot. What's wrong with me? How could I be so careless and leave those letters out? I don't need this drama right now. Vanessa should have never gone through my things. I stew to myself in silence until Jesse reemerges from his side.

"Look man, you can't beat yourself up too much. There's plenty of lonely nights ahead of you to do that later. Right now, you need to be focused on finding out if you are going to be a daddy soon. Women come and go, but you only get one chance to be a good father. Plus, women love single dads. When my mom and dad got divorced, my dad introduced me to like fifteen different step moms," Jesse says in attempts to comfort me.

"I know man, I remember. Your dad was always a smooth talker. But do you think that's why your parents got divorced?" I ask.

"Nah, actually I found out years later that it was my mother that wanted the divorce. She just was not in love with my pops anymore. She's much happier now, but my dad took it hard. He was really heart broken and he compensated by spending a lot of his time with new women. I wouldn't say he's depressed but I wouldn't recommend his lifestyle if you can avoid it. I just feel like he lost the love of his life and won't be content again." Jesse shared.

"Maybe. I'm not thinking about divorce, marriage, or anyone else right now. I'm not even sure if there's anything for me to do at this point. I'm hours away from Helen. Vanessa left as soon as she came. I kind of wish this day was just over." I sigh.

At that moment my phone rings. Could it be, Vanessa? No. Helen's calling me. I redirect my energy from Jesse to focus. I answer it as I am walking out of the room to gain some privacy.

"Hi Helen, everything alright?" I open up to her.

"I think so. I need to talk to you." Helen says with a soft voice.

"Sure, is it about the baby? I'm going to support you either way. I don't want you to worry. You're still my friend and you know I care about you. I don't want you to go through this alone."

"Oh really? What if it isn't yours?"

"This isn't about me. A baby is a baby. There's no reason for you to stress over genetics. Things happen. Sometimes we think we have it all planned but things go awry. Everything happens for a reason." I'm clearly speaking in third person to collect my own emotions.

"Aww, that's sweet. But you don't have to worry anymore about it. My period finally came."

"Sounds like you are relieved." I say disappointedly for some reason.

"Yeah, but that's not why I called. I just had a weird conversation with someone you may know. Do you know a Vanessa?"

(Gulp)

"Vanessa Williams? The singer?"

"No. Vanessa from your school. The one that sent me a friend request today."

(What in the flying flipping fuck! Could the day get any worse?)

"She's a friend." I defend.

"A friend you slept with apparently while we were together."

"How do you know that?"

"Oh, she told me. I didn't want to believe her, but by your reaction it must be true. She told me you two have been together since registration week."

"Why would she tell you that?"

"Why wouldn't you tell me that?" Helen questions my question.

"Why does that matter? You moved on from me already. A second ago I thought you were possibly knocked up with some other guy's kid."

"That was AFTER you broke up with me." Helen raises her voice.

"Right. And I broke up with you AFTER I slept with Vanessa because you deserve better. I didn't intend to hurt you. But I also didn't think you were just going to do the same thing to me."

"Oh really? You want to blame me for moving on from you? You really think what I did was the same thing? I should have never gotten back with you. I was a fool to think that you would wait for me like I was willing to wait for you. You were my first. Why didn't you just tell me the truth when we broke up?"

"What difference would it make? We aren't together. I'm not trying to argue with you right now."

"So, it's true."

"Yeah, it's true. But that's not really important. It didn't mean anything."

"I spent the last month wondering if it was my fault for letting things change between us. I cried for days before I told you about being pregnant. I felt like I betrayed you and the last two years of my life! A part of me felt that I was being punished." Helen reveals.

"Well, I'm sorry. But it seems like there's really nothing else to talk about then since you aren't pregnant. Whether I cheated or not is irrelevant. I didn't tell you for this very reason." I say hoping to divert her attacks.

"I just never thought you would be the one."

"The one what?"

"The one person I love, and the one person I hate the most. Good-bye, Aaron."

"Wait…"

She hangs up. With that silence I feel a rage take over. I cannot believe Vanessa! Who is she to think that Helen deserved to know? I call Vanessa next. She finally answers on the third call.

"Where are you?"

"I'm in my room. What do you want?"

"I'll be there in a second."

I race to her dorm in hopes to confront her for ruining my life. I firmly knock on the door resisting the urge to make a commotion. I'm red with frustration and sorrow. I can't wait to let her know that we are done. The door opens and Vanessa is there. Before I could even say my peace, I notice her.

Vanessa's eyes, sullen with redness and tears streaming down her face. She doesn't even want to look at me. I did not expect to see her so closely distant. My anger melts away into a stream of concern.

"Whoa, whoa, whoa… what's wrong Vanessa?" I plead to her.

"I don't want to talk to you. I promised myself to never be hurt again. Please just leave. I just want to be alone."

"How did I hurt you? I didn't go behind your back. I should be the one crying not you. Why are you so upset? What did Helen say? I know you spoke to her."

"I gave you the opportunity to let me talk to Helen. I don't need your permission to make my own decisions. I wish you would have told me sooner."

"What do you want me to tell you?"

"The truth, Aaron. Just the truth."

"The truth and *us* wouldn't have worked at the time."

"A lie and forever never works. You made me be a part of this. I recreated the situation I just left. Helen loved you so

125

much. Probably more than I loved my ex. Yet he cheated on me, and now you cheated on her."

"What do you mean forever?"

"I loved you Aaron. I loved you more than I thought I could love again. I wanted you to be different but you ended up being worse. How could you lie to someone like Helen and I expect you to treat me better? I don't want this anymore. Please just go."

"But I love you, too."

"Love doesn't work like this. You don't mean that. You love what we had. But what we had wasn't real. If you loved Helen and lied to her, who am I to compete?"

"What do you want me to do? I don't want to see you like this."

"Then it's best we just don't see each other at all."

Vanessa closes the door. I still hear her sobs from the other side of the wall. I place my forehead against the frame. I question everything I just said.

I love you? I don't even know who I am right now.

Chapter Twenty-Three

Backtracking

Mid-terms are here. In a week, I will be off for fall break to visit the family in Memphis. Vanessa and I haven't spoken since she broke things off with me. This was nearly a month ago. I would try to salvage some friendship with her but I doubt things could ever go back to the way they were. Ellis tells me he saw her with some new guy the other day. I guess you lose them as quickly as you win them. Honestly, between the two girls, Helen's words resonated more anyways. If I had just been honest with Vanessa, she would have never felt the need to confront Helen. Had I been honest with Helen, maybe I would have never let Vanessa into my life. I regret hurting Helen the way I did. She's right, I did cheat. I need to make things right.

"I'm sorry. I understand now how childish I was to lie to you. I won't make any more excuses. I don't expect you to respond, but I will be here if you change your mind." I send a text to Helen.

Passing through the humanities building I see a familiar face. Michelle is waiting for class to start outside the door. She smiles when she sees me. She's wearing sweat pants, a loose t-shirt, and a light jacket. He hair tied back in a bun, casually across the top of her head. She must have just gotten up for this class.

"Why look at you Ms. Dapper. It's mid-terms, not the Oscars. Did you have any time to study at all for the exam or did you spend all your time putting on make-up."

"Very funny Aaron. This is my only exam for the day. I don't need to impress you or anyone else for that matter. I hope your test skills are better than your jokes."

"Eh, it could be better."

"You're right, I doubt you could learn any more calculus."

"Oh, so you got the jokes today I see. Ha. How are you enjoying school so far? Can you believe it's already fall break?"

"I know right! I was planning on staying here for the break. My family is in Nashville, so I see them all the time. I rather just enjoy some peace and quiet for once."

"Yeah, that's not a bad idea. I wish I could get some peace of mind, too. My family's been missing me and I need to maintain some friendships while I have them back home."

"You got to feed the cats, otherwise they start to roam and never come back. My mom has lost a few that way," Michelle says with a smile.

I notice as we were talking, Vanessa is walking down the hall towards my side of the hall. I think she sees me. I turn to glance at her for a few seconds. The moment feels as if it was longer, but I recall biting the middle of my bottom lip to prevent showing any emotions. Vanessa walks into a classroom and then I return to Michelle's conversation.

"What are you going to do for a week to yourself?" I reenter.

"I will probably watch a lot of television and just organize my room. My boyfriend and I may be getting an apartment together, so we may look at properties for next semester."

"That's cool. I've thought about living off campus. Let me know how that goes."

The last student finally finishes their exam and shortly after the professor walks out. Dr. Dallas arrives perfectly on time with a briefcase full of papers. All of the students sit in assigned seats and each receive our copies of the test.

The exam consisted of 5 questions. One question to cover each chapter of our calculus book. It seemed pretty straightforward. When it comes to numbers or facts, I never hesitate. I write down the solution and derive the steps as I go. Either you know it or you don't. The last few weeks of being alone have given me plenty of time to focus on studies. If I wasn't studying, I was thinking about Helen. I miss the way she laughed at my jokes and held my arm during movies. She was my best friend. If only relationships were as simple as math problems. In about 45 minutes, I complete the exam and am the first to turn it in. Dr. Dallas seems surprised.

"Mr. Platypus, is this your final answer?"

"Were there more than 5 questions?"

"There will be more next time. Looks about right. Have a good fall break."

"Thanks sir, you too."

Michelle is right behind me with her exam in hand. She seems to be upset that I beat her to the front.

"You don't have to show off Aaron. Anyone can turn in a blank piece of paper." She jokes.

"If I wanted to take my time, I would have worn sweat pants."

Michelle scurries away towards the residence halls after leaving the building. She really doesn't care to deal with my foolishness. Turning in the exam gives me a calming feeling. Things are starting to finally feel normal again. Maybe my apology to Helen corrected the universe. I look at my phone and notice that she's texted me.

"Thank you. Maybe I overreacted. I didn't mean to say I hated you." Helen replied.

"It's okay. I deserved it. I'll be home next week. Maybe we can catch up?"

"I don't know, Aaron."

"It's just a few days. I should be home Thursday through Sunday. You don't have to decide now."

"I'll think about it."

I try not to push my luck, so I refrain from responding further to Helen. I can feel another weight lift from my shoulders. Maybe there's a chance for us to work things back out. People make mistakes all the time, I'm no different. I must have not understood what I had until it was gone. Helen was perfect. I scroll through my other messages and respond chronologically.

"Can you help me move next week? I know you'll be in town. We can catch up and I'll provide lunch." – Nicole

"Sure. I'll bring my dad's truck."

"Were you going to use your toilet paper?" – Jesse

"Why?"

"Hoops today?" – Ellis

"I'm down. After classes, around 5pm should be good."

A new message appears as I'm sending my reply to Ellis.

"Want to hang out next week when you are in town?" - Terri

"Depends. Helen tell you I was coming?"

"Yes. But she said she may be busy. I'm free though." Terri replied.

"Okay. Maybe. We can talk about it later. I still need to hang with Mark and Kurt."

"Leave Mark at home to his games."

"You still mad at him?"

"Wouldn't you be? He told me thank you when I said I loved him."

"Yikes. I guess it's better to love and lost than to love and be thanked."

"LOL. You were always the funny one in the group. Just think about it and let me know when you are in town."

More messages buzz into my phone.

"Thank You!!!" – Nicole

"Sounds good to me. Bring your roommate, too. His jumper is pretty good. He's usually wet from the perimeter." – Ellis

"Because I had tacos."-Jesse

"Fine. We hooping tonight. Ellis just texted me. Lace up around 5pm and we can head over to the rec center. I will grab more toilet paper from the student center on the way back to the dorm beforehand so I can change." I send to Jesse.

(Don't judge me. It's single ply tissue but it's free. They always stock the restrooms with extra. I just take what I need, I'm not greedy. I'm already taking out student loans and getting in debt. The last thing I need is to be wiping away my financial freedom.)

Chapter Twenty-Four

Find Another You

Finally, my exams are done for the week. I only have to pack before I go back home for fall break tomorrow. Jesse laces up his basketball shoes and wears his customary white tank top. He looks like a bum as usual, but don't let that fool you. He can "hoop hoop". For some reason the defense can never foul him hard enough to keep the ball out of his hands to lay into the basket. My role on the court is to play hard defense, set screens, and distract the opponent. I usually let others take the jump shots but I maintain all the trash talk. I can't seem to stop once I step on the hardwood—it's almost poetic the amount of nonsense I spew to get into people's heads. I check my phone to see that Helen has texted me back.

"You are in luck. I managed to get the day off Friday."

"Great! Hopefully that means I'll be able to see you."

"Sure. What did you have in mind?"

"We can go out to eat, grab a movie, then come by my house?"

"You don't think that would be awkward?"

"Why would it be?"

"Never mind. I'll see you then. What are you up to?"

"Jesse and I are about to play some basketball."

"Oh fun. Call me when you are done."

"I will."

Such great news. I am pretty excited to be able to see Helen. This just made my day.

"Hey Jesse, you ready to go?"

"Is water, wet?" Jesse confidently pronounces.

We arrive at the rec center and see that Ellis is already shooting around. He throws me the basketball as soon as I drop my bag off to the side.

"Bout time you showed up man. I was beginning to think you forgot where the gym was."

"I'm never late. I'm always on time. My time. You think we are going to find enough people interested in basketball during mid-terms?"

Not a moment too long after I asked, I notice a beautiful familiar face. And she's not alone. I guess she really did fine herself a new boy toy. Oh, and look, there's two busters on the side of him as well. He looks like a complete tool or maybe I am speaking out of jealousy. Her new man is tall and strong looking, like a 300-pound beef steak. I bet he can lift cars with his pinky. Either way, I'm sure she's noticed me, notice her with him; but Godzilla hasn't noticed that we've noticed each other. What does she see in this Mr. Swole with No Goals? I'm being too mean, he is probably a nice guy. Good for her, I guess.

"Vanessa just walked in the gym. You think she still mad at you?" Jesse calls out.

"Yeah I see. I don't know."

"What happened between you two? I thought that she was crazy about you."

"I guess we were both kind of crazy. It's all good. Let's just play."

"OK, but don't start missing your shots just because your ex is watching. She hasn't taken her eyes off you since she walked in," Ellis remarks.

"Man forget that. We here to hoop. This is the only shot I'm shooting today."

I throw up a brick. Bonk. A bit right of the rim and the ball ricochets close to Vanessa. Her new pet picks it up.

"You guys want to run threes?" the Oaf says to me.

Ellis and Jesse look at me to answer. I think they think I'm going to say no, just because of Vanessa.

"Yeah, let's play."

Immediately I see Jesse grin. Ellis shakes his head from side to side. He comes over to say, "Now we definitely got to win. But by the way you shooting, give me the ball."

The rules of pickup half-court basketball are:

1. First to Fifteen Points (15) by a margin of 2 or more. 3-point shots count as 2 points. Other shots count as 1 point.

2. Makers keep, if it changes possession you have to take it back behind the 3pt line before attempting a shot.

3. Fouls = Retained possession, no free throws. So foul away.

4. Contested possessions = Shoot for it. If you make it you keep.

5. Talk Trash, win or lose.

To keep things simple, we will call these folks New Guy and his friends #1 and #2. We got the ball first because Jesse made his shot. I take the ball from the top of the key. I can feel Vanessa's eyes staring at the back of my neck. The defense matched New Guy with me, Jesse with #1 (who was twice Jesse's size) and Ellis got #2 (a tall dude covered in what looks to be either tomato sauce or late puberty).

"You guys sure you want to match it up like this?" New Guy scoffs.

(Alright, I was rightful in my disdain. This guy's trash talking the wrong one. Let's play ball!)

First possession, I kick it out to Jesse and set up a screen for his defender, #1. His teammates fail to communicate. Jesse slithers pass after his guy collides into my chest, chin first. Swish! An easy 2-0 lead. New Guy and his cronies chuck it off as luck. Jesse then passes it to Ellis who calls for isolation. He doesn't want any of us to help with the screen. Tall #2 towers over him. Ellis lowers his shoulder and spins off his hip to easily lay up the ball on the other side of the rim.

"How you letting that short guy beat you to the rim? Man, you suck!" The Gargoyle complains.

"Don't disrespect my handles bro. He tall but can't ball." Ellis jests back.

I notice that New Guy appears to be taking us more seriously now. I bring the ball up to him and he tries to swat the ball from my handle. A rookie mistake on his part. I swing the ball behind my back and drive the opposite direction to make the layup. We are up 4-0 now.

"How you so jacked but can't score?" I tease.

That seemed to tick him off. Vanessa is looking on and watching for its reaction.

The score is now 8-1. Ellis slipped off Jesse's screen and the busters were able to scoop the loose ball and finally score one.

New Guy has the ball and checked it at the top of the key.

"I've been waiting to get the ball. Your lucks run out."

"About time. I was starting to think you guys never played basketball before. The goal is to score more points."

"You mean like this?" the New Guy jabs as he buries a three. I did not even contest it because he was so far back. Vanessa is audibly clapping louder than necessary.

"You got a cheerleader, don't you? That's cute." I mock.

He throws a hard chest pass at me to check the ball back. He must be out his damn mind, too. I get a little heated and now I am jawing even more during the game. It's one thing to get mad because you are losing, but to get mad because you can't talk trash—that's just pathetic.

After many failed shot attempts from the busters, the score is 13-5. But New Guy is refusing to give up to the odds. He seems to be playing as if his pride is on the line. Vanessa isn't clapping anymore.

"Look man. You ever need some pointers at basketball you can always search online for tips. They got videos you can watch. My little cousin just learned how to dribble. You can stand to gain something as well."

"Just inbound the ball already." he demands

"You sure? If I inbound it, the game will be over and you will have to wait your turn for a rematch."

"You got to win first." New Guy hopes.

"You mean like this?" I return the favor.

I fast pass the ball to Ellis on my left, cut towards the basket to draw in tweedle dee and tweedle dumb. They collapse and leave Jesse wide open. New Guy tries to cover their assignment. Jesse pulls up for the three. At the last second, New Guy gets his hand on Jesses forearm. You can see him slip off a puddle of sweat and fall to the ground. The basket is good for 2 points. On the floor New Guy is wailing in pain after rolling his ankle. I think I saw a tear roll down his eye. I feel kind of bad for egging him on now. Oh well.

By now, other challengers have emerged. After four more pickup games, we call it a night. I jet out a different way so I can take the longer walk home to call Helen. Jesse will probably want to hog the shower first anyways. There's no rush to race back. Helen seems to be in a cheery mood. She tells me that she's changing roles at her job and will be able to work from home. I didn't even know that was a thing. We talk as if we were right next to one another. It gets late, so I wish Helen good night after what seems to be an hour-long conversation. When I hang up, I notice a surprising text from Vanessa. I pause momentarily to read and reply.

"Wow. Was that necessary? I didn't know you could ball." - Vanessa

"There's a lot of things you don't know about me. Let's keep it that way."

"You're such a jerk. I hope I never find another you!"

Chapter Twenty-Five

Get a Grip

I managed to get home really early yesterday afternoon. I was anxious to see my family and friends. More importantly, I was excited to be able to see Helen again. I've missed the comforts that she brings—her caring eyes, soft hands, warm personality, and adorable smile. I realize that college is not an excuse to forget where home is and that home is wherever my heart longs to be. It's Thursday now, one day closer to Friday. Helen wasn't able to talk much last night after work, I figure she wants me to wait just a little longer more. That's okay. I don't mind waiting anymore. I have to help Nicole move today anyways, so I expect my patience to be able to withstand the wait.

Nicole is moving into her first apartment with one of our friends from high school. She's been planning this since she started going to college. Apparently, being grown at eighteen isn't the same as grown and on your own. Her parents don't seem to understand that college is almost a full-time job. We have to juggle friends, courses, study groups, and find time for romance. I'm out of town, so I can't imagine having to deal with my folks at the same time. In high school, they corralled us around and we really didn't do much beyond part-time jobs. But now that we are legal aged citizens, we can actually choose to do what we want. And with this new-found freedom, it's hard to go back home every day after dealing with college just to hear, "is your room clean, where were you last night, how come the Wi-Fi is broken?"

As I pull in to Nicole's driveway, I get a familiar wave from her parents. Nicole's whole family is out here to assist. I park and put on some work gloves before getting down from the truck.

"What's happening Aaron? How's school been treating you? I know you are probably about to graduate with that big head of yours. We always knew how smart you were." Nicole's dad says to me.

"Oh actually, sir, I'm about ready to drop out. These girls up there crazy and trying to trap a brother."

There's a long pause.

"I had the same problem, too, before I met Nicole's momma. My word of advice. 'Don't fight it. Embrace it! When you get to my age, you want to look back and be sure you did the right thing."

"I'm going to let you have that. I've only been there two months and I think I've seen enough."

We laugh it off together and Nicole finally appears from the front door.

"What did my dad say to you? I hope he isn't giving you bad advice again. Dad, I told you. Don't embarrass me in front of my friends."

"Aaron's not a friend. Friends bail on moving day. Family shows up on moving day. He can handle my jokes."

"Don't worry Nicole. Your dad was just saying I should live life to the fullest or else I may end up regretting it."

I wink over to her Dad. He gives me a solid fist bump.

"Whatever! Here, grab these last boxes and help me load the dressers. That's everything left from my bedroom. Then we can drive over to the new apartment. My roommate is already there unpacking."

We get in my truck and Nicole jumps in the passenger side. She left her car at her new home, knowing I was on the way with my truck. Nicole hasn't changed a bit and neither has our friendship. The last time we spoke was when Vanessa just broke up with me. Nicole puts down her phone, and as expected she interrogates me.

"So, Mr. Too Good to Call. What's been keeping you busy?"

"I knew you were going to bring that up. Honestly nothing much, just been focused on school."

"Just school? What about any crazy girls? Did you meet any one worth mentioning?"

"Actually, I've been trying to just make things better between Helen and me."

"Hold on. Stop the car."

"What? Did you forget something at home?"

"Yes, my mind! Because for a second, I must have misheard you say, 'You and Helen'."

"It's not like that Nicole. I feel bad that I hurt her and it's different now. I know what I want. It's her."

"Aaron. I say this because I love you like a brother. I am tired of seeing you get hurt. And if you think you should be with someone just because you've hurt them. Then you might as well keep hurting them. Because you'll never have any other reason to stay with them."

"Are you telling me I should just let her go?"

"I'm not telling you to do anything. But I'm letting you know that you are wasting your time with her. Did she tell you she wanted you back?"

"Well, after she found out about Vanessa, we weren't talking. She told me that I was the one person she loved and hated at the same time. She ignored me for a while but eventually after I apologized, we started talking again. We've made plans to see each other tomorrow."

"So, you don't know."

"I don't know. This is why I have to try. If she's happy without me then I guess that's how I'll leave it."

"I just don't see how you will be happy with her. Don't get me wrong. I like her as a person but I understand for us women—we have yet to grow into our future selves. She's going through these changes just as quickly as I am. I'm moving out of the nest for goodness sakes. Don't you think she needs to figure out her life, as well, before you guys settle back to your old selves?"

"I never even thought about it that way. I just figured she would want us to be back together. We only broke up because I was seeing Vanessa."

"That was the 2nd time y'all broke up. And here you are looking for break-up number three."

"Well enough about me... what's going on with you?"

"We can change the subject. But let me say this and I'll leave it alone. Regardless of whatever happened between you and Vanessa, nothing has changed between you and Helen. And that's not a good thing."

 "A part of me hopes you are wrong. But until I've tried, I don't know if I can agree just yet."

"You don't have to agree. But just be careful Aaron. I am tired of seeing you down and out. We have our whole lives ahead of us. Who knows, I may eventually find Mr. Right, too. But I'm focused on me right now."

As we unpack Nicole's things, I can't seem to shake her words. I know that I love Helen. And I am sure she loves me, too. But my mind questions if there is a greater love that I've yet to understand. Is love supposed to be this helpless, directionless feeling? Why does this love make me feel so powerless? After Nicole hugs me goodbye and thanks me for my help, I walk back to my truck. I hop into my seat and close the door. Listening to the faint ring of the dashboard before turning the key in the ignition. I turn on the car and let the engine idle. I take off my gloves and then head back home.

Chapter Twenty-Six

Letting Go

The day is finally here. I haven't seen Helen since the second breakup, a breakup I regret. At the time, I thought it was too easy. She pretty much agreed that we should be apart. If I had told her about Vanessa then, maybe I wouldn't be so sure now. I would probably be 2nd guessing if Vanessa would have been worth the risk. Now I know, nothing is worth losing your peace of mind. I spend this last month really kicking myself. I think I read every letter in that makeup tin box like ten times. I don't even know how those words even came to life. I literally spent hours a week just finding the right rhymes and syntax to tell Helen, "I love you". She always read them out loud when we were able to rendezvous after classes. Her voice seemed to complete my words.

"You're like the sun in the sky, the ocean by my feet—the way you move my world, I'm enamored and complete.

Your beauty radiates like a cosmic ray, cascading in the perpetual vastness of my gaze—my universe lives in you."

As poetic as I try to make this situation, I really don't know what words to say when I meet with Helen this time around. She didn't want to go anywhere, so I suggested we grab take-out and watch a movie in my room. She hesitated at first, I reassured her that my family would be home so there won't be any funny business. We compromised by agreeing to her choice of food. I would have been okay eating cereal at this point, anything to just see her again. My phone rings, Helen is calling to tell me to come outside my parent's house so we can ride together. I can feel my heart pounding like a drum in my chest. Even though I've been ready for this call for days, I still can't believe she's outside waiting for me.

I walk out the front door and lock it behind me. Trying to pretend this is just any ordinary evening with Helen. I take my time walking to her car to mask any of my anxiety. I open the passenger door and take a seat, prioritizing my seat belt before I said hello.

"Hi Helen."

"Hi"

She looks absolutely flawless. I can tell she's put in some thought into this moment as well.

"So... where do you want to eat? My treat." I offer.

"We can grab some sushi. Don't worry, I can pay for myself."

"Well at least let me pay for the soy sauce."

"Don't you have that at home already?"

"Yeah, it's free for you. I won't charge you for it."

She smiles.

"You're still silly."

We arrive to the restaurant and place our orders to-go. They estimate a 15-minute wait. The tables inside are all full. It was a good idea for takeout. Helen and I sit beside the front door as we wait.

"So, tell me about school. Do you like it?"

"It's going. I don't really have any complaints. Jesse and I are making good friends. Classes are going okay. How about you? How are you liking work?"

"They keep giving me more responsibilities, but I think it's fun. I get to set my own hours now and there's opportunities for growth. I'm still learning, but you get used to it."

"Do you plan on being there a while?"

"I'm not planning anything. Just going with the flow."

"I see. Well thanks again for spending your day off with me. I know there's probably a million other things you could be doing."

"Don't overthink it. I wasn't busy. You were in town, I wanted to see you, too."

My anxiety is alleviated. I wish Nicole were here to hear this. Sounds like Helen does want us to be together.

"I really am sorry, Helen, for ruining things between us. I was afraid I lost you as my friend."

"We will always be friends, Aaron. I just don't think we should be more than that."

(Well, my acid reflux is back.)

"What do you mean?"

"I realize that I can't hate you. I can't hate you for living your life, as I should be living mine. But I can still be your friend. I still value the happiness we've had together."

"I see." I murmur.

I really don't know what to say right now. I was hoping to claw my way back into Helen's heart. But she's built a fortitude around it, labeled "friend zone". The lady calls us upfront to pay for our food.

"Is this separate or together?"

"Separate" we both declare simultaneously. The room seems to go silent as we stare at one another.

In the car ride back to my house, I stare outside the window in silence. It's obvious that I'm upset. My eyes feel heavy but I refuse to cry in front of her.

"Aaron, what's wrong?"

"Nothing. I'm just thinking."

"Well, what are you thinking about?"

"I don't know."

"Are you upset about us being just friends?"

"Partly. I just wasn't expecting that response. I know I messed up. I was hoping to fix things between us."

"There's nothing to fix, Aaron."

"Then why do I get the feeling that we should still be together?"

"What would be different if we were together?"

"I wouldn't feel alone anymore. I wouldn't feel guilty anymore."

"You don't think I feel those things? I'm not trying to feel that way either. But us being together won't fix that for you. I'm not trying to be difficult. I've been doing a lot of self-reflection. I'm not sure what I want. And to be honest, I do love you, Aaron. I was mad before, when I heard about Vanessa. But I wasn't mad that it happened. I was more concerned with why you didn't tell me yourself."

"Because I was a fool. I figured you would rather not know."

"Aaron, I'm not trying to blame you. I'm just saying—are we meant to be if we don't trust one another?"

"How do we trust each other again?"

"Just be my friend. Support me as you would someone you loved without needing love in return."

"I can't calm my heart. Even now, I feel as if my life would be nothing without you."

"I know, Aaron. I'm still there with you. But what difference would it make in 3 days when you are away again? We won't be physically together."

She's right. And she usually is when it comes to my emotions. I feel like this is a test. I've been trying to forcefully do this my way. I should just try this from her perspective. We arrive at my house. We continue to sit outside in the driveway.

"You're right. But I still love you. My desire is for you to be happy. If this is what will make you happy. Then that's what I want for us, too." I reply.

She breaths a long sigh of relief. I hold her hand. My thumb caressing her palm. She lets out a tear.

"This will be the last one."

"What do you m---" I almost say.

She kisses me before I can complete my sentence. Her lips melt away my pain. I open my eyes and she is smiling.

"Thank you, Aaron, for coming home to see me. I am really glad that we had this conversation."

"Let's not worry about it. No crying! The food is getting cold. I'm always going to be here for you."

We go inside to eat, but Helen doesn't stay long after we finish our food. She and Terri made plans to go out later. She hugs me goodbye. Helen's thin frame is pressed against my chest. Her scent fills my lungs with fond memories. I silently pray this moment never ends. I look into her eyes and embrace her for a little while longer. She gives me a small smirk to read. I take it that it's time to let her go.

Chapter Twenty-Seven

Newness

Back at college, it's a new week with different happenings. It was good to see Kurt and Mark over the weekend. We just hit up the skating rink and kicked it as usual. As much as I want to tell them about my romantic life—it is never the time or place with them. The most we share are just details on which girls we smash, not which girls we love. Emotions are a complicated mechanism for the guys. As brothers we tend to know exactly how we feel without anything being shared. But we suppress most of what needs to be said. Mark never falls in love. Kurt is always going 100 miles per hour. I tend to be the one that was always consistent, up until Helen and I broke up. Now I feel like I'm going back and forth between women. I won't go into too many details but I couldn't rely on my own advice—so I tried listening to others.

This was around Halloween. A bunch of the Greek organizations were throwing toga parties and costume events. I went as Prince from Purple Rain. Jesse wrote thug life on his belly and went out as Tupac. Jesse was happy to be able to not wear clothes in public and it not be frowned upon. At a frat house I met this one student. She was clearly batting her eyes towards me. She asked me if I wanted to bless her in the waters of Lake Minnetonka. I was not expecting things to go there so quickly again. But I had been drinking more than usual to hide my somberness. We dated for a few weeks off and on. But ultimately, I couldn't keep messing with her. She was the opposite of Helen. She was aggressive, desperate, and wild. She wanted to get married and have kids like yesterday. I lied and told her I was anti-marriage and had a vasectomy when I was twelve. She was fun while *I* lasted.

Then in November I met one of the nicest people ever. She had the sweetest laugh and was angelic. I felt inadequate beside her. I made her laugh one day while passing in the halls and we started to chat some more. Come to find out, she was a very devout religious person. I found it refreshing in this day and age. (Maybe my lifestyle has been causing my own pain and I needed to return to a holier state.) Everything seemed to be going according to plan—butterflies in our stomachs, text messages throughout the day, and we even started eating lunch together when our schedules matched. This was until she found out I wasn't a virgin. She judged me before she even met me. I couldn't stand it. How could you blame me for my actions before we ever met? It was unfair but I didn't fight to keep her. I have been doing just fine in my own state of hell.

Over Christmas, a high school friend reached out to me. She was a little bit older so I honestly don't remember her from school. Apparently, she had been interested in me since my junior year whenever Helen and I first started dating. We grew close enough for us to exchange gifts. Albeit, my gift I got from Best Buy. She gave me the gift of sex. Around new year's she ignored all my calls. After a week, she finally tells me that she's sorry for ghosting on me. I let her know that we should just be friends. She seemed delighted. I wasn't bothered because I was already eyeing my next valentine.

This girl was a track star. I caught up with her on one of my morning runs. I saw her wink and smile at me as I was tying my shoe laces. I chased her for nearly 2 miles before she let me get her name. She told me I could get her number at the end of her jog. Ten miles later she turned around to see that I was not there anymore. I understand you have to work for love, but I am not going to kill myself for it. The last time I went on a run with a girl, she broke up with me. I just think it's a bad omen to start a romance this way. Maybe I should have stuck it out a little longer because the next girl was crazy.

Jesse told me about this girl in the adjacent dorms. He said that she just transferred here this semester from a community college nearby. She was as hot as he described. She looked better than Vanessa! Jesse told me she was stuck up though. She didn't pay him any attention, but she likes to flirt with a lot of jocks. Typically, I would not pursue the cheerleader type but she actually pursued me. I ran into her at the library and she was working on some algebra problems. Without flirting, I helped her and was trying to get back to my own studies. She made me wait so we could exchange numbers. I was very surprised. I assumed she just wanted to have a personal tutor on hand whenever she needed help again. She texted me her room number and the only division I did involve her legs. I forgot everything that made me love Helen so much. But things were too good to be true. The next evening, she texted me this long drawn out letter about how she didn't want to be in a relationship with anyone. "She's new here and that she wants to focus on school." I showed it to Ellis and he had the same text message in his phone from her. This girl had a playbook on conquering men. I never felt any less special in my life.

I just can't do this anymore. I don't know what Nicole or Jesse's dads were thinking. Playing the field is leaving me with a lot of muddy shoes. I can only tread so far before it gets exhausting. It's almost summer and I really need a break. None of these girls even compare to Helen. I rather just be alone and focus on myself over the summer. That was until I got a text from Terri.

"I'm mad at you!" She blasts my phone.

"Who is this?" I coyfully respond.

"You know exactly who this is."

"What do you want Terri?"

"It's been almost a year since graduation. And you have yet to call or write."

"I didn't know you were waiting for an invitation to call me."

"Well, there's three months in the summer. I don't want any more excuses. I heard you will be interning in Memphis."

"Yeah, so I may be busy. Don't get mad at me for trying to make it out of the hood."

"Boy! You were on the Chess team. You aren't hood."

"You can always hang out with Mark. He's home."

"Enough about Mark. I know he's your friend, but him and I will never get back together. I see myself with you more than him."

"Yeah, I know what you mean. But Mark is my best friend. We are more alike than you think."

"How about when you get back, you try me."

"If I wasn't such a nerd, I would assume you are asking me out on a date."

"You can call it what you want."

"Are you joking? Aren't you and Helen best friends?"

"She doesn't have to know. I'm tired of dating around. I know how nice things were with you and her. I'm sorry things ended how they did. But she seems to be happier with her new guy. You deserve better."

"What new guy?"

"You didn't know? She's engaged. I thought she told me she told you."

"Naw. That's news to me."

Chapter Twenty-Eight

Running in Circles

I've been waiting for Helen to confirm the news, I am too gun shy to confront her. I don't know what to believe. If Terri is telling the truth, then that means Helen and I aren't as good of friends as I wanted us to be. Why wouldn't she tell me? If Terri is lying, then I would be making a fool of myself. I don't control Helen. Yet she seems to have my every emotion on a string. This was two weeks ago when I found out. But how long has it been? How do you even meet someone so quickly and accept a proposal? We are only 19 years old. The last girl that asked me for a baby was trying to settle down, too. I turned her away because I figured that would be insane. Am I the crazy one?

I'm back home in Memphis for the summer and I'm not quite sure if I want to be here any longer. I only accepted the internship at my old job because it was an easy way to be close to home without appearing desperate. I should have applied somewhere else, anywhere else. I want to know but at the same time I feel like I already know it's true. Fuck it, I'm going to call her. The phone rings four times before the voicemail nearly answers.

"Hello? Aaron?"

"Why didn't you tell me?" I begin.

"I was going to but I just wasn't ready to tell you. How did you find out?" She asks with disbelief.

"We are supposed to be friends. This is something friends wouldn't keep from one another."

"Why? We're still friends."

"I don't think we can be. Friends don't hurt one another this much."

"This is supposed to be one of the happiest moments in my life. Why can't you just be happy for me, Aaron? I want you to be happy."

"If it were that simple, I would be. I got to go. I just needed to know for myself. Oh, and by the way. Terri wants me to go out with her. I'm sure that won't be a problem?"

"Really?"

"I just figured you should know. I'll talk to you later."

"That's not fair Aaron. I really like this guy."

"I would hope so! I really got to go. Mark and Kurt are here now. Congratulations." I end the call as badly as I wanted to make the call.

I open my front door and see Mark and Kurt brought over tacos. They had their arms stretched out with a choreographed hello, up until they saw my face.

"Heyyyy… whoa. What's wrong Aaron?"

"Sorry guys. It's nothing. Come on in."

"Doesn't look like nothing. We missed you too but you don't see us crying. What happened?"

"I thought I was over her. Helen got engaged. I thought we still had time to work things out."

"Well I guess no Street Fighter tonight." Mark says

"Sorry Mark. We can still play I just need a minute to figure it out."

"What's there to figure out? She's with another dude. You should just let her go. Her and Terri are just alike. Terri was always trying to mess around with the next best thing. That's why I never took our relationship serious. She tried so hard to make us like you and Helen. My forehead not that big. How can she ask me to be like you?"

"Terri was the one that told me Helen got engaged. This was before she asked me out on a date." I respond.

"When you got friends like that, why have enemies? Damn Aaron. No wonder she never replied to my texts. She was sprung on you!" Kurt responds.

"Don't worry. The last thing I want right now is to be with anyone that reminds me of Helen."

"No what I'm saying is, before we graduated—she never gave me the chance. I wouldn't be surprised if she was the one that got Helen to break up with you in the first place."

"Helen and I broke up because she was worried that I would move on while in college."

"Didn't you do just that?"

"That's only because I felt like something was missing. I thought we were perfect. I realize now that is far from reality."

"Bro. These two have brought you more misery than joy. Let them have their day in the sun. Some people aren't in love. They are just in love with the thought of being in love." Mark eloquently states.

"I wish I could move on as fast as you do Mark."

"I don't move on quickly. I just don't get involved quickly. I got my heart broken a long time ago in 2nd grade. My first crush embarrassed me. She married me on the playground on Monday. On Wednesday I saw her marrying this other dude. It was real to me. From then on I promised myself to do better."

"You were seven!"

"And? We nineteen now. It only takes one heartbreak to know you don't want that shit again."

"You make a valid point."

"It's easy to get upset. It's hard to move on. But you don't owe them anything. There is no happily ever after," Mark says

"Who says she and this guy will work out anyways?" Kurt asks.

"I'm not going to hold my breath for a divorce."

"Good. Now eat these tacos before I combo your ass." Mark demands me to get it together.

"Put up or shut up then." I declare.

We set up the game and I wipe my tears away. The conversation's mood turned from serious to silly. I really needed that from my friends. As much as I want to stay angry, Mark's words were right. This is my first heartbreak. It's painful. I can feel my chest cave in and the air from my lungs thin with each beat. Every ten seconds I think about Helen and her white dress. I had this vision of being the one waiting for her to walk down the aisle. Now that dream is tainted. I wish it were me, but I can no longer see myself standing in front of her. The evening continues with Kurt and Mark tag teaming in Super Smash Brothers on the Nintendo. Mark takes his opponent head on and Kurt distracts his guy by running in circles.

Chapter Twenty-Nine

Rebound

Throughout the summer, I spend most of my free time lifting weights. The moments of solidarity within the gym challenging myself, takes my mind off of the past. I want to grow past my former self. Maybe if I become some physique god, it would win back Helen. I want her to regret letting me go. It's an unhealthy obsession with the gym. I've started working out 5 times a week and weighing my food portions. I cut my body fat percentage down to 12% over the three months. Every time Helen texts me what I'm doing, I just share a selfie from the gym or the scenery of my hike. She seems to enjoy how passionate I've become about my health. We avoid talking about her wedding plans or feelings. I think it's understood that it wouldn't be healthy for our friendship. I'm not sure why we even talk. We only text.

The week leading into school's return, Ellis reaches out to me. He wants to workout at the gym and see if my basketball skills are still polished. I suggest we lift before we hoop. He likes the idea. As soon as we rendezvous at the fitness center, I hear Ellis call my name.

"Damn Liu Kang! Is that you, Aaron?"

"In the flesh." I say with my arms stretched out. I purposely wear a tank top to reveal my chiseled biceps and molded physique.

"Did you eat a horse or something? When did you get so big?"

"Just been eating right and staying consistent. I'm not that big. Still 180 pounds"

"Yeah, but you were 180 when I met you. You a solid 180 now."

"Yeah. I will probably stick to this size. I don't want to get any bigger."

"I should lift with you more often."

During the lift, we focus on mainly pulling exercises. Deadlifts, rows, pull-ups, and some ab workouts. Ellis struggles to keep up but is enjoying pace. He notices that a few girls our age have been staring in our direction. He suggests we go over to talk to them.

"Aaron, they looking at you. Help me introduce myself."

"I'm good man. I just want to finish the workout."

"Well I'm trying to get my workout in too. My eye, neck, and pelvis workout. Just walk over there and say hi."

"You can. I'm not trying to talk to anyone right now. Besides, we still got three more sets."

"If you say so, bro. But if they come over here, I'm going to need you to be my wingman."

Sure enough, the two girls walk over and ask if we were finished with our set. Ellis offers them the machine and say we can all workout together. He introduces both of us to them. I stay focused on my workout. Ellis looks at me with pleading eyes to be more cordial. The girls grow tired of us and after the set they move on to a different area.

"Dude! She was waiting on you to talk to her. She must think we are a couple or something."

"Sorry Ellis. I'm just not in the mood for small talk or romance."

"What's wrong?"

"I feel like I deserve to be alone right now. My ex is getting married and to be honest, I'm miserable."

"You mean the girl from high school? Dang that was quick."

"That's what I thought."

"Look man. I get that you feel maybe you deserve to be alone. But you are choosing to be alone. There's nothing wrong with being alone. I've been single for a long time. You don't see me moping around."

"Have you ever been in love before?"

"I'm in love right now!"

"I'm flattered but I like women. We still cool though."

"No, Aaron. I love myself. I love that I am who God made me to be. I have faith that things are the way that they should be. There's a bigger purpose for each of us. We can't rely on our own plans."

"What if God is punishing me for my sins?"

"Then ask for forgiveness and move on. The first step is to remove that sin from your world."

"I have. I'm focused on me. I haven't cheated on anyone, because I am not with anyone. I've been patient."

"Sin isn't just an action that you do. Sin is a circumstance. You are living in Hell over Helen."

"Come on man, she's still my friend."

"Would a friend put you through this over and over again? She may not be trying to hurt you, but it hurts you to be around her. You got to stop talking to her."

"Like completely?"

"Completely. You are one of my best friends. It shouldn't be a constant roller coaster to maintain our friendship. I haven't seen you in months and we are still close. If Helen is truly meant to be a positive influence in your life, she will understand."

"I think you're right. Every time I get a text from her, I race to see her message. I always withhold my true feelings. Everything is one-sided. I have to pretend to be happy. I just want to be happy."

"And that's not a selfish request. That is all we can ask for ourselves."

"What do I do in the meanwhile?"

"Talk to other people. Read a book. Sleep. Anything you want to do. You got to focus on other things."

"I'll try it. But if I am tempted to text her. Do you mind if I text you instead? I need someone to keep me honest."

"Only if you be my wingman for reals next time. Just because I'm single doesn't mean I ain't looking. I need to be selfish, too!"

My phone buzzes almost serendipitously. Sure enough, it was Helen checking in. She knows I work out at this time and it's just before her lunch break.

"You ready to go back to school?" – Helen

Ellis looks at me wondering if I have short term memory issues. I delete the text. He gives my shoulder a shake of accomplishment. "Now that wasn't so hard was it?" I sigh and feel somewhat relieved. We put down the weights and head toward the gym to play basketball. As we walk in, a loose rebound ends up at my feet. One of the girls from earlier steps in front of me to retrieve the ball. I hold on to the ball for a second.

"You want to play 2-on-2 with my friend Ellis?"

Chapter Thirty

Good Friends

Sophomore year, I accumulated over 32 credit hours. I'm on pace to graduate by my fourth year. It's surreal how quickly time flies. I remember just moving in to the dorms—now I'm watching fresh faces wander the campus. Was I this wet behind the ears? I have my classes printed and walk to the bookstore to purchase my required textbooks. There's quite a long line in the humanities and business sections. I move around them and collect my science books. Michelle is here as well. She's already wearing sweatpants.

"Is that who I think it is?"

"Aaron! You always catch me at a bad time."

"What do you mean? This is primetime for you. What's the special occasion for the new digs?"

"I don't have time for this. Let me just grab my books and go."

"Well dang. I'm just welcoming you back to school. I can't miss my favorite calculus buddy?"

"Don't brag about beating me on the final. You got lucky."

"It's not a competition. We both got A's in the class. How was your summer?"

"Pretty bad actually. I broke up with my boyfriend. He cheated on me over the summer."

"I'm sorry. I didn't know. Are you alright?"

"Yeah. I'm better. It's just been a rough month. I still need to find a new place to move by next week."

"Well, if you need any help, I have a truck."

"Thanks, I got some friends that are helping me though."

"Well at least let me carry your books back for you. Do you want to get some coffee? You look tired."

"Sure."

We checkout at the front. I notice that she and I have some overlapping classes. Physics, Organic Chemistry, and Anatomy Lab. Michelle thinks I must be stalking her. I joke that she's the reason I did so well on the final. She is mildly annoyed. As we walk out of the bookstore, I can feel the weight of her books bending my back in half. I resist wincing in front of her. I don't normally go out my way to be this nice. But I feel a sense of guilt for when I cheated on Helen. I can't fix my broken heart, but I can at least help Michelle get through hers. We walk out of the student union and stop for some coffee by the library where she is parked. I drop off her books in the trunk. She orders a white chocolate mocha; I grab a caramel macchiato. In return for the coffee, Michelle offers me a ride back to my dorm.

In her car, it looks disheveled with empty straw wrappers, coffee cups, and notebooks. She tells me to get in and ignore the mess.

"Thanks for the coffee. You really didn't have to carry all the books by yourself." Michelle applauds.

"Don't worry about it. You just saved me a workout for the day." I boast.

"Don't let your ego inflate too much, Aaron. I can't imagine that head getting any bigger."

"I'll let you get in one joke since you've had a bad month."

"Bad is an understatement. I found out over Facebook that he was cheating. He was tagged in a photo with some random girl. When I asked him about it, he got really defensive and didn't want to directly answer my question. That's when I knew he was cheating."

"Wow. Speaking as a guy, he probably was." I say in third person.

"I just feel so stupid. Why did I move in with him? Now I have to deal with separating all our stuff and he keeps wanting to apologize."

I feel like Karma is making me relive my mistakes. This must be how it was for Helen when she found out about me. I wish I had known what I know now, back then. I continue to give Michelle the comfort I think I would need to hear if I were in her shoes.

"Don't blame yourself. It's not your fault. It's better to see things for what they are now, rather than later."

"What am I going to do? I still love him."

"You can love someone without being with them. If it requires so much effort to love a person, is it really love?"

"I guess not. I just wish I could get over him."

"Have you tried focusing on yourself? Not communicating with him? Learning to be alone?"

"What do you mean learn to be alone?"

"I'm single. And that's okay. I've been in love before. But right now, I'm trying to learn how to love myself more. I'm learning new things about myself every day. I just learned that I hate the way they made this coffee."

"To be honest, I never expected to be alone. That's what hurts the most. And there's so much of his stuff I have to pack."

"Being alone allows you to be selfish. You never have to worry about not getting what you want. As hard as it may be to understand now, it's better to be alone than to be with someone who hurts you. Make him pack his own stuff."

"He doesn't want me to move. But everything in that apartment reminds me of what we used to have. I don't want to be in it anymore."

Michelle's statement reminds me of Helen's letters, the letters that I shredded. After not speaking to her for months, I figured she would have forgotten me. Helen sent me an invitation to her wedding. The invitation had typed faced font embossed on the outside. The card was sealed in a pink envelope with a golden seal. "You are cordially invited to attend the ceremony of Helen Jameson and Michael Edwards. December 14th at Merrion Country Club." Helen wrote a personal memo on the invitation.

"Aaron, I don't know where in the world you are right now. But I would love to have you attend. I want you to know that I'm happy and I want you to be happy. Your friend, Helen."

I thought I would have been fine, but seeing a date to our end, crushed me. It took everything I had to keep myself faithful to my promise. As bad as I wanted to call her then, I chose to shred the invitation and the letters of our past instead. I return back to Michelle's voice.

"Then don't. You got to do what's best for you. You can't keep going in circles. You'll end back up where you are now." I reclaim.

"What if I deserved it?"

"No one deserves to be unhappy. But if we allow others to make us unhappy, we are choosing to be unhappy."

"Sounds like you've been through this before."

"Somewhat. I know someone who has."

"What did they do?"

"They didn't wait. They moved on. They didn't ask for permission to be happy. They just are."

Michelle wipes her eyes and hugs me tightly. I pat her shoulder and let her know things will be okay. She recomposes herself as I pull away from the unexpected emotions. As I leave her vehicle, Michelle says, "Thank you, Aaron. I'm glad I talked to you. You're a good friend."

Chapter Thirty-One

Telepathy

"Should I go?"

"I am. Free food. It will be fun. You shouldn't worry," Nicole convinces me.

"What if I don't go?"

"We can always leave early. Mark, Jesse, and Kurt all got invitations. It can be like an early high school reunion."

"As long as you guys are with me, I'll go. I won't do anything crazy."

"I'd hope not. Please don't be that guy who objects during a wedding. That's how people get shot."

"Alright. I'll see you there tomorrow."

"Don't forget to bring a gift! I got them some nice dinner plates off their registry."

"I have to buy a gift and not object during the wedding? Helen's asking for too much!" I sarcastically say.

"A gift card will be sufficient, Aaron."

"Alright. Good night."

I pretend to get some sleep. I find myself lying in bed retracing memories into the ceiling with my eyes. I forget how I even got up to eat breakfast. My parents think I'm over stressed by school and tell me to drink some tea. It does help a lot. Soothing, warm infused water heightens my senses, yet calms my mind. I reach out to the guys in a group text to see if they are getting gifts, too.

"What did y'all get for wedding gifts?"

"I bought them a pack of socks. But I wrapped it up really nice." – Mark

"What gift?" – Jesse

"Gift card" – Kurt

"How much was the gift card?"

"$20."

"Cool, I'll get a gift card after I leave the gym. See you at five!"

"Don't do any chin ups unless you outdoors. Big forehead ass will break the ceiling." – Mark

The weather today is sunny and surprisingly pleasant. The temperature is in the mid-sixties and you can get away with wearing shorts. I fix my crooked tie to snug tightly up against my collar, as tightly as my biceps hug these sleeves. Then I tuck my shirt into my newly purchased dress pants. The custom-tailored, non-pleated silk pants crops at the middle of my ankle. My black leather oxfords reduce the formality of my appearance and bring my frame square to my wide shoulders. I feel very confident and strong as I face my mirror. I accentuate the look with my suit coat. I keep it classic with a black suit, white shirt, and black tie.

At the country club, I see rows of cars neatly parked beside one another. I see Helen's car parked beside one side of the building. Neatly dressed friends and family are migrating to the entrance. I would suppose over two hundred people are here. I'm not sure who all these people even are. At the registration table, I see some familiar faces. Helen's family seem to be surprised to see me. They don't recognize me at first but I can hear the whispers after I sign the registry. AARON PLATTENBURG in all capital letters. I navigate the maze of gazes and search for my friends. I find the row where Nicole saved me a seat. The whole gang is there to greet me. This isn't so bad.

We wait for half an hour before the audience begins to get impatient. People are starting to voice their concerns for how late it's getting. My phone buzzes.

"We can't find Helen." – Terri

"What do you mean? Why are you texting me?"

"Do you know where she may be?"

"No. I've been sitting in the audience. I haven't seen her. Get the groom to look for her."

"It's bad luck for the groom to see her before the wedding."

179

"It's bad luck to lose the bride before the wedding, too."

"We've looked all over the building. She said she was going to the restroom. Her car's still here. We know she didn't leave."

Nicole, Mark, and Kurt can't believe what's going on. Jesse takes this cue as a sign to lose the suit. He strips down to a short sleeve dress shirt and starts heading towards the reception tables.

"Where are you going, Jesse?" Kurt asks.

"If the wedding is off, I'm still going to make me a plate. I didn't come here to leave hungry." Jesse says without a whisper.

The room's air is filled with a gasp of silence. The wedding coordinator tries her best to take control of the situation, but everyone is in disbelief. Before the room gets any louder, I leave towards the parking lot. Nicole, Mark, and Kurt don't notice. People are pulling out their phones to gossip online.

I walk directly to Helen's car. I knock on the tinted windows to get them to roll down. There she is in her white dress, sobbing with tears and surprised to see me.

"Aaron? How did you know I was here?"

"You invited me. This is your wedding day."

"I wasn't expecting you to come. Where's Michael?"

"Still standing at the altar waiting for you. Let's go."

"I'm not ready to go."

I climb into the car and close the door. Sitting beside her and watching her cry doesn't stir any good memories within me.

"Does anyone else know that I'm here?" She asks.

"No, I just had a hunch you would be in your car."

"What hunch?"

"Well, we broke up in my car. I figure that's your go-to space when you are feeling alone."

"I shouldn't feel alone. I just think I'm making a mistake."

"What mistake?"

"I just don't want to get divorced. How do I know that this marriage will last?"

"Did you ever think we would break up?"

"No."

"Did that stop you from dating me?"

"Dating and marriage are two different things."

"Not really. It takes trust. It takes compromise. It takes faith."

"So why did we not work out?"

"We didn't trust one another. I didn't want to make it work when things got hard. I took the easy way out. I stopped believing."

"I'm sorry, Aaron."

"It's okay, Helen. I wouldn't be here if I still had any hard feelings."

"What should I do?"

"Do what makes you happy. Does Michael fulfill you? But more importantly, are you fulfilled?"

"Yes. He's a great person. I'm so embarrassed. He probably hates me."

"I doubt it. He's still at the altar. He hasn't moved. He's unnerved. He trusts you will be there to meet him. So, let's go."

I grab Helen's hand and drag her towards the ceremony. She's wiping her tears and begins to laugh. Terri and the other bridesmaids grab Helen to quickly regroup in the dressing room. I grab Jesse from the buffet bar and tell him to put his coat back on.

Back at our seats, Canon in D starts to play and people silence their conversations. I see the groom standing beside his best man at the front of the ceremony. He is fighting back tears. The flower girls are Helen's younger cousins. The awes erase any memory of the delay. Bridesmaids paired with groomsmen walk in succession. Terri's eyes focus on me as she passes by and I can see her jaw dropping. I duck my face to ignore her advances. By now the music stops and the *wedding march* resonates in the room.

Everyone is at their feet. Helen is standing alone, clutching her bouquet, eyes veiled, and her train tracing her steps. Her newly applied makeup masks her tears from earlier. As she walks by my row, she pauses a moment to let me admire her face. I see a single tear roll down her cheek which she wipes away quickly. Without a word being said, I can tell she's reassured herself of this decision. Helen continues down the aisle to meet her husband.

Chapter Thirty-Two

I Know Her

I'm late to physics lab. Michelle is probably wondering where I am. She had to do last week's experiment by herself because we traded assignments on P-Chem lab. The cohort we started with has shrunk. This demanding major has thinned the herd. Michelle and I ended up taking several of the same classes. It was her idea for us to start studying together once she trusted my study habits. Or maybe it was because I could make the same A as her, while telling jokes.

"Aaron! You're going to do all of the demo at the end. I've already had to set this thing up by myself."

"What is this?"

"It's an oscilloscope."

"It looks like a radar detector. All you did was hook up two leads and turned it on."

"Yeah, well it took a lot longer than it should if I had had help."

"Fine."

We spend the next hour and a half measuring different currents and voltages with the multimeter and characterizing the wave forms. We are the last ones to leave the lab. All of the other stations are empty by the time we wrap up the experiment. Even though Michelle said I would have to clean up alone, she sticks around to help.

"Are we still on for studying later?" She wants to know.

"I can come to the library for a little bit. I need to get ready to go out with Ellis." I tell her.

"That's fine. Where are you going?"

"Ellis wants me to go on a double date with him at the only Italian restaurant nearby. He met someone the other day and needs me to be the wingman."

"Oh. Are you excited?"

"Not really. Blind dates aren't my thing. Come to think of it, I'm not sure if dating is my thing. I can't remember the last good date I've had."

"Don't be so hard on yourself. I'm sure you are a good date."

"You tell me."

"What…?"

"I'll come to the library dressed up. You let me know if I look decent or not."

"I'm not sure if I would be the best judge. I'm perfectly content in sweat pants."

"Yeah. At least you have a variety of colors to pick from. Guys have to try to be fancy. Women could show up to a date naked and it would go well. That I know."

"Please wear pants when you come to the library."

"Damn. Now I got change my whole outfit."

"Alright. Well... see you later. I'll save us a study room on the second floor."

"See ya."

(Pro-tip for going on a date with someone new: Eat before the date so you actually spend time talking to the person. And this saves money because you end up ordering less food.)

A few hours later, I head over to the library. I walk upstairs and find Michelle buried in a textbook. I knock on the door and barge in before she looks up.

"Ma'am, we can hear you snoring. Can you keep it down?!"

"Aaron! Oh my god you scared the crap out of me."

"The look on your face is worth it."

"I thought you said you had a date tonight."

"I do."

"You didn't even change from this afternoon."

"Exactly. No need to change perfection. If she doesn't want me for the real me, she can pay for her own dinner."

"Did you run this by Ellis? Aren't you supposed to be helping him look better?"

"I am. If I look better than him, it wouldn't make a good impression. I'm not going to take criticism from you and your Michelle Mondays sweat pants."

"I don't know why I study with you."

"Because it's either me or the other folks in our major. You know—the ones that think they know it all and have no personality."

"I hate it when you are right. One of them asked me out the other day. I think he sneezed in his hand right before he shook my hand."

"And all this time I thought you were a prude."

"I didn't know until after he shook my hand!"

I think we spent more time talking than actually studying. I only had an hour or so before Ellis came to get me from the library. Michelle seems to be much more comfortable with me now than she was two years ago. My jokes are actually welcomed. She seems glad and isn't too bummed about her ex-boyfriend anymore. She ended up getting her own place and brand-new furniture. Brand new heavy ass furniture that I ended up moving because her previous help was unreliable. I always joke about how she owes me lunch but I never cash in.

(Ellis knocks on our study room door.)

Michelle scoots her chair away from me suddenly.

"Sorry, don't mean to disturb. But Aaron, we got to go."

"You in a rush ain't it?"

"Dude, you not gonna change clothes?"

"For what?"

"You just wearing basketball shorts and a sweater. Never mind. I don't know why I expected more."

"It's not too late to ask Jesse to play wingman."

"No. You're right. Sorry Michelle to take away your study buddy."

"I was getting bored with him anyways. I don't even think he studies otherwise if I wasn't here." Michelle remarks

Ellis and I make our way to the parking lot where he's parked in the back. As we are walking, he gives me a devilish grin.

"You better not have set me up on a date with Shrek."

"No. It's not that. I don't know what your date looks like. My girl told me she looked good."

"So why do you have that look on your face?"

"Man, you didn't see how Michelle was all up on you?"

"Huh? Michelle? She was reading the chapter with me. I forgot to bring my textbook."

"Sure. She was damn near sitting in your lap."

"That's not funny. She's just a friend."

"Well you could have fooled me. Why don't you talk to her? She doesn't look bad. You guys are always together."

"If she wanted to talk to me, she would try harder. I don't think I've ever seen her dress up. She and I just study together that's all."

"If you say so. When was the last time you went on a date?"

"I don't know. Last semester I think."

"See! You've been out the game too long. You don't recognize when someone is flirting with you."

"I've been out the game too long? I taught you the game!"

"Well the student has become the master, young grasshopper."

"Whatever, you should be glad I didn't dress up. I would be taking your girl."

"Don't play about that. I really like this one."

"This is like the only person I've ever seen you date."

"Yes. I really like her."

"I won't do anything stupid. But if my date is crazy, I'm walking home."

We arrive at the restaurant where Ellis hugs his new lady. I don't think they are official or anything, this is probably date number 2 or 3 for him. Normally Ellis doesn't go for seconds because he is extremely picky. Her name is Sandy and she's a delightful person. Sandy says her friend just went to the restroom and will be right out. Apparently, Sandy's friend must have been nervous to go on a blind date. The host calls our attention to say our booth is ready while tucking the menus into her arms. I stand up to look around for my date and there is Vanessa. Sandy introduces her to me as we didn't know one another.

Chapter Thirty-Three

Worthy

I turn and head for the door. Walking back towards the campus. Ellis runs after me.

"Where you going Aaron?"

"I'm walking home!"

"Stop playing man. Come back inside. They are going to give away our table. You're killing me man"

"Did you know Vanessa was her friend?"

"No. I didn't. You don't have to like her. Just hang out and be cool."

"If I had known she would be here, I would have worn pants."

"Why are you trying to impress her?"

"She's my ex. I forgot she even went to school here. I've done good hiding in the library. I rather she not know how I am doing or if she does know, know that I am better off without her."

"It's just food. Please come back inside."

"If she brings up any bullshit from last year, I'm out. And I mean anything."

"I'm pretty sure she's forgotten. Man, other guys would be bending over backwards to be on a blind date with her. You act like she's ugly or something."

"Looks aren't everything. I just feel like this date is a waste of my time."

"Be nice."

Back in the restaurant, I play it coy with Vanessa for Ellis's sake.

"Vanessa! Girl… is that you? Long time no see. I thought you died."

"No, I didn't die. You're the one that's a ghost."

"I didn't know that you guys met." Sandy says.

"They used to date." Ellis mentions with a look of spite.

"I wouldn't say date. Vanessa and I were in love…" I defend myself, creating a long pause at the dinner table.

"…she was in love with herself and I was in love with myself."

Vanessa doesn't find the comment very funny. The waiter arrives at the perfect time to take the attention off of me.

"Why isn't this a lovely gathering. Double date?"

"Alcoholics anonymous." I interject.

Vanessa fights back a smile.

"Ignore him. Can we have some water for the table and some calamari?" Ellis orders.

"And two trays of breadsticks please." I request for Vanessa.

"Right away, I'll come back for your orders shortly."

"Don't think that make us good friends again, Aaron."
Vanessa quirks at me.

"Them breadsticks ain't for you! Just kidding. You can have mine if that helps."

Vanessa and I bicker back and forth for about twenty minutes. We failed to notice Ellis and Sandy leave the table together. They haven't return.

"Where did they go?" Vanessa asks

"I don't know. Didn't you ride with her?"

"No, I drove."

"Didn't you ride with Ellis?"

"Yeah. I guess I'm walking home."

"I'll give you a ride."

"You don't have to. It's only a 2-mile walk. I could use the exercise."

"You could use a donut. Where were all these muscles last year?"

"In repair. We ate out too much, Vanessa. And we spent most of our free time having sex."

She blushes.

"Aaron! You have no shame. Keep it down."

"Am I wrong?"

"No. It wasn't that simple. Aren't you still talking to Helen?

"Are you still talking to Popsicle Stick Ankles? I return her questioning.

"No. We broke up a long time ago. I haven't been with anyone serious since."

"Well, Helen got married."

"Really? I assume not to you."

"It's fine. She found a good guy. If you are wondering if I am single, the answer is yes."

"I'm sorry to hear that, Aaron."

"Sorry, for what? I'm not down about it."

"I guess I figured you be more upset. I know I would be if my ex got married before me, even though I hate the guy."

"Life is not a competition. It's a journey. We all get to the same destination one way or the other."

"That's one way to put it. Your M.O. was to always be strong minded."

"Naw, that's just my B.O."

Vanessa laughs.

We have no idea where Ellis and Sandy went, but I suppose we deserved to get ditched. I didn't know we would still argue so much after all this time. But right now, things seem okay. Vanessa is even more beautiful than I remember. I did not know that was even possible. She's straightened her hair and applied her makeup. It's new to me to see her in this light. Seeing Ellis involved with someone makes me a bit jealous. I was usually the one going on dates or chasing something new. Maybe I was really running away this whole time? Vanessa's presence makes me wonder too much.

"I guess it is time to leave. Did you get enough breadsticks?"

"There can never be enough." She clarifies.

"Where's the waiter with the bill?"

"Don't worry about it. I already paid it."

"When? You really didn't have to."

"It's fine. It was between you stuffing your face with dessert and the time I had to go to the restroom."

"Well I hope you don't think I owe you anything."

"You don't. I appreciate you keeping me company."

We gather our things and make way to her car. Vanessa stands beside me. I don't know why, but I grab her hand. She doesn't pull away. I feel her fingers lace mine. I think she's missed me a little bit.

"Are you sure we should be holding hands?"

"It's cold. You're warm. What's the big deal?"

"I don't know if we would work again."

"You girls talk too much."

"That's my line!"

"I know. So, what do you wanna do?"

"Maybe we should try again. But slower."

"I'm okay with that. Dinner was fun, I guess tiramisu is off the table."

"Don't push your luck."

We get back to the dorms' parking lot and she turns off her car. I lean over and press my lips against hers. She stutters to say nothing. I feel a sense of nostalgia with her. Her familiar skin and scent calm my insecurities. This kiss is more honest. I feel no reservations and neither does she.

"Good night, Vanessa." I say after puckering off her saliva from my lips.

She hugs me while resting her earlobe on my chest. From this distance I can embrace all of her details. And considering all of her qualities, I'm not sure I deserved a second chance.

Chapter Thirty-Four

Impatience

"I can't be with you." Those were the last words Vanessa
told me before summer break. I walked away and never
looked back as I packed my things into the truck. I'm not
going to play games with Vanessa anymore. She tells me that
not being together is better in the long run. Apparently, she
believes that I will cheat on her over the summer and would
rather not know the truth. She controls the narrative. If we
aren't together, I can't prove her wrong or right. It's whatever
at this point. I have other things to do with my life. If she
wants to hold last year against me, she can be my guest. I'm
not even a nymphomaniac, but I won't be withheld just
because she thinks it ruined our relationship the first time
around. I didn't even bother to argue with her. I'm so glad to
be going home.

New summer, new internship, same city. Memphis is
home for me. I remember moving here as a kid and being the
only Asian kid in my class. Everyone was so nice to me and
wanted to learn how to say my name. I met Kurt and Mark in
6th grade and we've been best friends ever since. I'm learning
new things about home every time I visit. Beale Street isn't
just famous for the live music and delicious food—it's become

a Mecca for us kids catapulting into adulthood. There's decent barbecue and then there's real Memphis BBQ. I took it all for granted when I left for college. Not anymore! This summer I'm focused on the things that make me happy. I am Aaron Plattenburg.

It's the beginning of July, so I have an extended weekend off. My only plans today are to practice my guitar, write some new songs, and eat ice cream. I got the guitar as a gift to myself last Christmas. After Helen's wedding, I began to wonder what to do with my free time because the gym was getting old. You can only lift so much before you risk bursting blood vessels. I fell in love with the sunburst acoustic guitar, the moment I saw it. It reminded me of my journey from where I was a year or so ago. The dark brim of the wood is engulfed by the center flames. The rosewood fretboard and raised frets callus my fingertips every weekend. I've gotten good enough to write, play, and sing my own songs—albeit it I can't sing very well.

An unexpected buzz rings my phone. This better not be Vanessa.

"Are you home?" Michelle texts. I call her back to speed up our conversation.

"Did you mean to text me?"

"Yes. Are you home?"

"I'm at my parent's house in Memphis."

"I know that silly. I thought you were smart. I'm in Memphis."

"Oh. What are you doing here?"

"I am visiting a friend. But he has to work and won't be off until seven. What is there to do here?"

"There's a bunch of places to eat. It's too early to go downtown. What are you trying to do?"

"I really don't even know why I am here. If I had known the guy would be busy, I would have waited to drive down from Nashville."

"Oh. Well, if you want, you can come hang out with me. I'm just hanging out in my room."

"Ok. That sounds fun. Text me your address. I'm near Poplar and by Walnut Grove."

"Well that's about fifteen minutes from me. See you soon."

I have the entire house to myself. My parents are visiting some friends. My brothers are out doing their thing. So much for a relaxing day to myself. I spend the next few minutes tidying up and wait for her arrival. I could not have predicted the next chain of events.

Michelle struggles to know where she can park her car. I watch her nearly take out my mailbox. Once I see that she's exiting her car, I walk away from my blinds to act natural. I've never seen Michelle outside of school, let alone did I ever expect her to visit me in Memphis. She was always a book worm or too busy to hang out if it wasn't school related. She rings the doorbell with a slight delay. When I open the door, the Michelle I expected was nowhere to be found.

In front me stood a woman with long brown hair, lightly highlighted ends, loosely waving down her shoulders. Her eyes were green and cerulean with a golden shimmer. She wore a fitted red shirt with sleeves barely tracing her semi-sculpted delts. Long slender arms with porcelain skin, encapsulated with shiny French tip nails. Her hips hugged her dark brown shorts, that stopped before the middle of the thighs. Plain blue open toed sandals covered the ground as she stepped closer to me. She looked amazing. I may be drooling a little.

"Hi Aaron!" Michelle says with a smile. I barely snap out of my trance.

"Hi, Mi mi Michelle." I stutter while inviting her inside.

"You have a nice house. I like the decorations."

"Yep. This is my house."

"Are you home alone?"

"Yep. The house is lonely." I can't seem to form sentences for some reason. Why is Michelle making me so nervous? When did she get so beautiful? Is this the power of sweatpants?

"Well, thank you anyways for letting me come by. I really don't know where I am going around here, and I didn't feel comfortable driving aimlessly."

"No problem. So, you are here for a guy friend? Like a boyfriend?"

"No. Maybe. I don't know. But he's at work so I guess I'm just here with you for now."

"Where's your stuff?"

"I left it at his apartment."

"Oh ok. Cool. Well I didn't have any plans. I was just practicing my guitar and watching TV."

"You play the guitar?"

"I wouldn't call it playing. More like, I'm learning."

"Do you take lessons?"

"I'm teaching myself. Internet videos are amazing. We live in a great day and age."

"That's pretty impressive. I don't expect anything less though from you."

"Aww, if I didn't know any better, I'd think that was a compliment."

"Good to know you haven't gotten a sense of humor. Play me something."

I lead Michelle up the stairs to my empty room. I realize there isn't much space to entertain so I commandeer my brother's room. She's even cuter in a smaller setting. She sits beside me on the bed as I pretend to tune my guitar. I admire her in my peripheral vision. At first, I play some covers from a few notable artists: John Mayer, Al Green, and Musiq Soulchild song snippets, only the parts that I am comfortable singing. Michelle seems to be enjoying my renditions. She lays her head on the pillow as I continue to play. I grow more comfortable in this new zone with her.

"Do you have any original songs?" She asks while curling up closer to the pillow and my bent knee.

"A few. But they aren't any good. Just some things I wrote to a tune."

"That's how most songs start. Come on. Play me another song. Don't keep waiting again."

"Every day

Baby, look I'm tired of the dreams that you give me.

I know that you're real but you're not here with me.

And is it wrong to want to feel your touch and your smile.

Please don't make me wait for long, because I've been here for a while.

And it's like, every day I'm thinking about your face.

And it's like every day I'm trying to find the words to say.

And every day I'm holding back from telling you that…

You're so beautiful. You're so beautiful to me, baby.

You're like my sun in my sky, the ocean by my feet.

And it's so soothing how your love's affecting me.

I wouldn't change one aspect or one flaw.

Because you're so perfect in my eyes through it all.

And it's like every day I'm thinking about your face.

And it's like every day I'm trying to find the words to say.

And every day I'm holding back from telling you that…

You're so beautiful. You're so beautiful to me, baby."

I put my guitar down and lay beside Michelle. We stare at the ceiling together. She seems to be speechless.

"Did you really write that?"

"Yeah."

"Who's it about?"

"I don't know. It's just a song."

"People don't just write songs like that."

"Well I didn't write it. I probably lived it. I just felt like making a song about it."

I perch myself up beside her and look over her face. She covers her mouth instinctively.

"What are you doing?" Michelle asks.

"May I kiss you?" I plead.

"Umm... I guess?"

At first, she keeps her hands placed over her lips. I kiss the back of her wrist and feel how soft her skin is for the first time. She giggles and slowly moves her hands down to her chin. I meet her top lip first and take my time leaping across the gap of her mouth. I can hear her exhale disbelief in between that moment. Her wintergreen breath tastes as good as it smells. She pushes the gum to the side of her mouth as my tongue wrestles hers. I catch my own breath but she grabs the back of my head to restrain me. She kisses me back once more before letting out a giggle.

"Where did this come from, Aaron?"

"If I knew, I would have kissed you sooner."

"Do you always kiss your friends?"

"No. I just felt that the moment was there. Was I wrong?"

"I don't know what came over me either."

 Michelle's phone buzzes and her face fills with disappointment.

"What is it?"

"My guy friend is off work early. His boss is letting him go home."

"Stay here with me. I can sleep in the other room."

"My stuff's over at his place. It would be rude for me to go get it just to leave. He doesn't go to school with us. I only came here to visit him."

"Do you like him?"

"I think I do. But right now, I don't know what I like."

"I like you. I feel that you may feel the same way."

"I know. I just don't know what to do about this guy. If I had known this would happen, sooner, I would have just come to see you. I better leave before it gets too late. I'll text you later."

    She kisses me again and smiles. I watch her gather her things and reminisce about her lips mentally, imagining ways to keep her here longer. Ultimately, she leads me to my front door and leaves without me. I spend the evening waiting for a text that never comes.

Chapter Thirty-Five

Technical Knockout

I woke up that next morning very late, wondering if yesterday was a dream. Michelle still hasn't reached out to me. Did I just lose another friend? I didn't expect to kiss her yesterday. Then again, when do you expect to kiss anyone? I'm going to have to deal with her looking at me weird every day now in our classes. Really smooth move, Aaron. My cell phone disrupts my self-loathing.

"Can I come over again?" Michelle texts.

"Yes. I was beginning to wonder where were you."

"Sorry, I got busy last night. And I didn't have a chance to text you."

"That's fine. Feel free to come by anytime. I don't have any plans."

"Okay. I'll stop by before heading back to Nashville. But only for a little bit. No funny business, Aaron."

"I have no sense of humor remember?"

I take her lack of a response to mean she is racing her way over here or maybe she's blocked my number. Maybe I should text "lol". I send it, but it's met with silence. Did I just fuck things up again? I begin to pace my house for the next half hour pretending to be cool.

Luckily, she did show up. And she looked just as good as yesterday. Why can't I shake the feeling of butterflies? I've seen pretty girls before. It's too early to fall in love. Even she said we were just friends. Now she's at my door again. I open it before she can knock. I'm somewhat afraid to draw any attention to the guests I bring over.

"Hi Aaron."

"Hi Michelle. Long time no see."

"Goof. Let's go to your room to talk."

"Umm... my brother is asleep in that room. We can talk in the guest room if you want."

"Wherever is fine. No need to get your guitar this time."

I point her in the direction of the guest room and follow her. I'm noticing how beautifully thick her legs are; hidden all this time behind a curtain of loose cotton. Her exposed legs contract and relax with each step; some moments pressing against each other rippling a supple bounce. I forget to pick my jaw off the floor when she turns to face me. She sits on the edge of the bed opposite of me.

"Kiss me again." She demands.

"Why? I want to, but tell me why first."

"I'm trying to see something."

I kiss her without further hesitation. Her eyes stay closed long after I leave her lips. I can tell she wanted more.

"I thought about you last night."

"Then why didn't you text?"

"Because…"

"Because you were with another guy?"

"Not just that."

"I suppose you weren't in a position to text."

"Yeah. I didn't expect that to happen last night either."

"I'm not going to judge. If you didn't leave when you did— maybe it would have been me."

"I was thinking about you during."

"Thanks…I guess? I kind of lobbed you to him. Sorry it sounds like he wasted your time."

"We are supposed to be just friends, Aaron."

"We are. We can be more if you want. If you don't, then we don't."

"Is it that easy for you?"

"Far from the contrary, Michelle."

"I don't want a relationship right now."

"I want whatever it is you want."

"I want you on top of me, like yesterday."

This time I don't waste any time talking. I get as far as unbuttoning her shirt. She stops me before I could unfasten her pink, silk, padded bra.

"Not today. You are going to have to wait."

"Until when?" I whisper before exploring her clavicle.

"When I know you've earned it."

"How do I earn it?"

"If I told you how, then you could never earn it."

"But you gave your guy friend some yesterday. Did he earn it?"

"That was meaningless."

My heart beat stops.

"What happened to being just friends?"

"We aren't just friends. We were lab partners. We're study buddies. And now we're about to cross the line. A little wait should not be too much to ask."

"You're right. Just be careful what you wish for."

"What do you mean?"

I grab her by her thighs and quickly skirt my grip over her panty line. She gasps in exhilaration and surprise. Then I place her hand on my abs.

"Alright. You can go. If you leave now, you can make it home before 3 o'clock."

"You think you are so clever. This is my test. You can't torment me with my own rules."

"I've been without sex for months. You just had some yesterday. I think I can hold off for even longer. I'm used to it now." I say and wink towards her.

"Dammit it, Aaron."

Michelle is smiling as she redresses herself. I walk her out to her car and kiss her one last time for that summer. We talk nearly every day leading up to the start of our junior year of college. We talk about sweet nothings and rearrange our class schedules to spend even more time together. We aren't in a relationship, but it definitely feels like one. The nightly video chats feel as if our faces were touching again. I mark the day I will see her again on my calendar. We agree that by then, I would have earned it.

The Saturday night before classes, Michelle's just gotten in town. She's had time to prepare her apartment for my arrival. I was at the gym unaware of her texts demanding my presence. She is "tired" of making me wait.

"I want you, Aaron. Don't make me wait any more. Come over now."

"I need to shower first and I still have another set of exercises to do."

"I don't care. Exercise me. You can shower over here." She insists.

"And if I say no?"

"Then I will just start without you. I won't have time to open the door once I get started."

"Okay. Since you put it that way. I'm coming!"

"Not before me."

I race over to her place. I think I ran two red lights. Fortunately, there was no traffic to avoid. She opens the door for me and is as absolutely flawless as I recall. She is only wearing a bath robe and grabs me by my sweaty collar to quickly hide me inside. She throws me a towel and tells me to hurry. I clean up before the fun starts. I make due with her cucumber melon bodywash and fruit scented shampoo. I rush to cut off the water after the soap is rinsed from my derriere. I enter Michelle's room and see that she's skipping the foreplay. Her bathrobe is hanging on the computer chair.

I gawk at how exquisite her frame draws all of my attention. I climb on the bed and she is excited to embrace my back with her legs. I never knew a woman's touch could be so amazing. I underestimated her control over me. As badly as I wanted to impress her, I forgot how long it has been since I've had sex. I can still hear the shower draining in the tub by the time I lost my stamina. Michelle's excitement and luring eyes quickly transform into a look of disappointment. I try to salvage the situation.

"Round 2?" I awkwardly propose.

"Umm... No."

Chapter Thirty-Six

Masquerade

"Welcome to Organic Chemistry. I am your Professor, Dr. Boson. As you can hear from my accent, I am not from around these parts. I am from New Zealand, not Australia. If you've made it this far into the depths of chemistry, you must be either pre-med or a fool. Take it from me, I took the academic route, my colleagues all smell like toluene. I just smell like ethanol. You guys and gals call it Blue Top Vodka on weekends." The professor recycles his class introduction.

By now, I've gotten use to the professors spending hours enjoying the sounds of their own voice. I would skip the lectures if they didn't take attendance for us to keep our scholarships. I also come to class hoping Michelle talks to me again. She hasn't said a word to me since last Saturday. The most I've gotten from her is a smile and eyebrow raise goodbye. I'm the one that should be embarrassed. She's covered her beautiful body again in her usual attire. I'm still deeply enchanted by her presence. I sit a seat behind Michelle but it feels like a mile apart right now. I text her to see if she'll respond.

"Hey, can we talk about last Saturday." I buzz to her phone.

She looks down at her phone but doesn't respond. My heart breaks a little. The class period is cut short for the first day and I wait to get up from my desk. I want to time it to where Michelle and I can walk together without it being too obvious.

"Can you please talk to me." I say beside her in the halls.

"This isn't the time."

"I'm not trying to make this weird. I just don't understand why you're being silent towards me."

"It's weird now, Aaron. I was afraid of this."

"It doesn't have to be weird. I've known you since my first day of class. Why does it have to be weird?"

"You've seen me naked. I've seen you naked. And now I have to see you three times out of the day."

"But I've also seen you cry. I've seen you laugh. I've seen you smile. There's more to us than just last Saturday."

"Aaron, I need some space. That's all. We can be friends and not talk about it."

"Well talk to me then. Talk about anything else."

"What do you want to talk about?"

"You got any plans this week?"

"I'm going to see my friend in Memphis."

"Really?!" I burst in surprise.

"Goodbye, Aaron. I'll see you later."

Michelle turns another direction leaving me with little answers on how I can repair what seems to be broken. I'm so angry at myself for getting emotional. She's not my girlfriend, but I feel like I've been dumped. I need to cool off. I make my way down to the engineering college basement to grab a drink from the vending machine. Reaching down into my pockets, I see that I am ten cents short. Surprisingly, a familiar voice offers me her charity. I feel like a bum.

"Here." Vanessa says while handing me a dime.

"Thanks…" I grab my soda can and turn to face her.

"So, how was your summer?" Vanessa asks.

"It was good. Like any other summer. Yours?"

"I went back home. It was hot, but I was able to relax."

"Cool. Are you still staying in the dorms?"

"Nope. I finally moved off campus this year. It's been good so far. My roommate and I got a two-bedroom apartment. You should come by and see it."

"Cool. We'll see. I got to go. Thanks for the dime."

I head over to the library to wait for my next class. I try to listen to music and pass the time, but my eyes fixate on my phone's screen. I read through the texts from Michelle over the summer. I miss talking to her every day. As I scroll through the past month's messages, a new message notification pops up.

"Did you think about me over the summer? Not that I thought of you or anything." – Vanessa

"What do you want me to say?" I reply.

"I don't know. Seeing you today made me think about some things."

"Like what?"

"How lonely my summer was and how it was nice seeing you again."

"That's what you wanted, remember? Don't tell me you're having second thoughts."

"What do you want?"

I ponder for a second to answer her question. I haven't thought of what it is I actually want. I want to redo Saturday night with Michelle. I can't believe myself. I'm such an amateur.

"I want to see your new place."

She texts me her address paired with a smiley face. We make plans to hang out later in the week.

Knowing that Michelle wouldn't be in town this weekend, I decided to count my losses and move on. I've been here before. I refuse to be the man on the side. If I am going to be miserable, I should find some company. Why else would Vanessa be handing me loose change?

Later that week, I go to Vanessa's place. Vanessa's apartment is much more inviting than her dorm room. She has her own space with a door to keep us confined to share the same air. Vanessa thinks the summer apart grew us closer. I simply go through the motions of our pleasantries to find an escape between her thighs. She's been reluctant to let me reenter that world of hers even though she badly wants me. too.

"Aaron, we can't just start where we left off."

"So why am I over here?"

"Because I enjoy your company."

"Well, we can multitask."

"Very funny. But no. I want you to wait a little longer. As much as I've missed you, I want us to enjoy being friends for a little longer."

"You've always been the one to set the rules."

"I don't mean to tease. I just think we owe it to one another after all these years."

Hearing the words "these years" makes me realize that I've known Vanessa as long as I've known Michelle. But I don't think there's anything more for me to learn about Vanessa. I don't know why Vanessa wants me to wait and see how our relationship can grow. The only thing she grows for me is the bulge in my pants. I don't like for this to be my only desire. I know that I desire more from a partner. All the while Vanessa's lips caress my neck; I think of how Michelle makes Vanessa pale in comparison. I'm numb to her kisses. I slowly pull away.

"Fine. I need to leave anyways. I got to hoop with Ellis and Jesse in the morning." I lie to getaway.

Vanessa thinks that I'm disappointed, but I'm really not. I just want to be alone. I give her a kiss to reassure her that it's not her. Vanessa's lips are still sweet to kiss. She gives me a small peck on my cheek as well before I leave for home. I don't know how much longer I can carry on this façade.

Chapter Thirty-Seven

Tell me

As badly as I feel I deserve a second opportunity to impress Michelle, I've learned that you can't force these situations. The year has only begun and I am more than willing to wait for her. I love the way she plops down in her seat in front of me in class and smiles at me. I live for those two seconds every morning. Then I go back to pretending not be bothered anymore by our lack of conversation. She asked for space, I will respect her wishes. Even though it's almost September, it feels like yesterday when she arrived at my doorstep.

I usually reminisce about her every day alone, but this particular day was a Friday. I was heading downstairs from the fourth-floor elevator after class when I saw her wave to me to hold the door. I hesitated at first but eventually stuck my arm out to let Michelle in. There we were again. Alone, silent, and my heart still. I was afraid to speak; as if my words would ruin the moment. A moment for us just to be together again.

"So… how's it going?" Michelle opens up to me.

"Good. Been really busy lately. How about you?"

"I'm making it. This year seems to be more science classes than the years before."

"Yeah and the classes are smaller now. We used to have sixty people take chemistry with us. Now it's just you, me, and the other four lab coats."

"What have you been up to besides classes?"

"Nothing really. Just playing my guitar, basketball, and hanging out with some friends."

"Oh yeah, you and your guitar."

"Nothing's change for me. I'm still me."

"You write any new songs?" She subtly pries for more details of my well-being.

"I'm always writing new songs. But lately, I've been wanting to rewrite an old song."

"Maybe I could give it another listen."

"I'd like that."

"I'm free this weekend. Bring a textbook so we can study together. I see now that things between us won't be so weird."

"I tried telling you. But you and your sweatpants are so stubborn."

"I'm used to being alone, Aaron. Guys for me are simply an escape. I felt like you were becoming another escape. I don't want you to leave that way. And I admit that studying by myself this month has been lonely."

"Using me for my brains."

"I mean… that's all you're good for," She jokes with a blushing smile.

"So, you got jokes again. It's not my fault you were so loose. I couldn't control myself."

"What? Loose? That doesn't make sense."

"Don't be so loose next time."

"Who says there will be a next time?" She quibbles.

The elevator door opens back up to the fourth floor. We never moved because neither of us hit a button. The person is expecting us to exit. We get out and decide to take the stairs down instead to avoid the embarrassment. She laughs with me as we continue to make our plans for the evening.

I would be lying if I said I wasn't more nervous this time around coming over to Michelle's place. I wasn't even sure if she was serious about me bringing over my guitar to play for her. I brought every textbook in case she wanted to change the subject. I do one final check in the rearview mirror to make sure I look decent. I can see the sun setting in the background. This time I text Michelle before knocking on her door. She replies instantly to come on in.

FRIENDS, LOVERS, OR NOTHING

Inside, I throw my backpack down beside the couch and set my laptop on the coffee table. She gives me a surprising look. I realize that she has put out chocolates and an assortment of romance movies to pick.

"Aaron. It's Friday night. I didn't call you over here to study."

"Then why didn't you tell me that before I hauled all of these books over?"

"You are terrible at this."

"Terrible at what?"

"Knowing when a girl still likes you."

"It's hard to tell when the person asks for space and pretends things never happened."

"Most guys would chase me longer. You kind of floated away."

"You seemed to be seeing someone else anyways."

"Girls like it when you fight over them."

"I don't want to fight over anyone. I've had that before. I refuse to be second best."

"Am I not worth pursuing?"

"You are worth every moment that I've thought of you. I would pursue you as long as you wanted me. But I will not fight over you. The Michelle *I want* reciprocates my feelings, and would not expect me to make her fight for me."

"Aaron…"

"If you want to play games, I'll let you play by yourself."

"Why are you making me choose between having fun and us still being friends? You can do the same thing."

"Who says that I am not? I can be your friend. But I won't be your lover as well. I can have that with other people."

"Are there other people?" She asks surprisingly.

"Why does that even matter? You have your friend. I have mine as well. The only difference is, I'd rather have you."

"I didn't know you were seeing someone else."

"How could you know? You won't talk to me. And now today you act like I haven't been missing you all this time."

"I thought I still had time to figure out what I wanted. Who is she?"

"She's an ex, but we still talk. Do you even want to be with me?"

"Yes, I do."

"Then just say that."

"How can I be sure you are the right choice?"

I kiss her and stare into her eyes holding back my tears.

"Because I won't let myself lose you again. Michelle, I never realized how incomplete my world's been until I found you in it."

"Aaron. You don't know me as well as you think. I have baggage. I am afraid to get hurt and I am terrible with commitments. It never ends well."

"What do you feel when I kiss you?"

"I don't really know. Fear, passion, silence, peace, honesty, confusion…"

"When I kiss you. I feel you. And I feel who I want to become through you. I've never felt this way before. I've been with a lot of people—none of them like you."

"Aaron…"

"What is it?"

"Stop talking." She says and shuts my mouth closed with her lips.

She pushes me towards her room while I backpedal without leaving her embrace. My arms get tangled as I race to take off my shirt. She helps me with my belt and pants after she's kicked off her shoes and sweatpants. On top of the bed she's straddled me with only her panties and shirt remaining. I reverse her onto her back to begin our voyage.

Finally, Michelle allows me to redeem myself. I leave no inch of her unexplored. We lose ourselves to each other that night, and the next night, and the next night. Monday morning, I wake up beside her with absolute certainty that she is the one. She opens her eyes as I run my hand through her hair.

"Good morning." I whisper in her ear.

"How long have you been awake, Aaron?"

"Long enough to make breakfast and clean up the kitchen."

"You're so sweet. I've been meaning to tell you something."

"What is it?"

"I do want to be with you.

Chapter Thirty-Eight

Honey

It's true what they say. "Good things come to those who wait." I can sense our bond growing by the day. Michelle has been more open to me as the weeks go on. She even holds my hands in between classes. Our classmates notice that we are dating and seem to approve. We never needed their permission, but it is nice to have their blessing. I notice that Michelle's retired the sweatpants. I think the daily breakfast I cook, gives her the energy to try a little harder. I love watching her get dressed. Every morning, I discover how evolved her style actually has been all this time. She's beautiful in every way. Whether she's in pants, dresses, shorts, or nothing at all.

One particular night, we had a study date planned in the library. I left class early to fetch a room before other people could book it. I walk over and notice that there are only a few available rooms. One is reserved with chairs filled with unaccompanied backpacks. The other is empty, so I quickly enter and set down my things. There are six chairs, a table, whiteboard, and a monitor to hook up a laptop. I rearrange the room to make space for food, Michelle's things, and my computer. As I retrieve my charge cable, I hear Vanessa knocking on the door. Her voice raises the hairs on my neck in surprise. I sit down after getting a good look at her expectedly gorgeous face. I try to hide any impulsive reactions in my shorts. Vanessa's outfitted in a low cropped t-shirt and tight blue denim shorts. She casually has a jacket wrapped around her waist to hide her plump ass and silky toned legs. She smells good, too. Her fragrance is a mix of body lotions and perfume that is perfectly suited for her smile. She sits right beside me. I think she can smell my arousal. Her feet are nearly touching mine.

"Mr. Plattenburg, I see you are still a student around here. Where have you been hiding?"

"Vanessa. Yes, I still managed to stay enrolled. I've been keeping myself out of trouble. I see you are dressed for a job interview. What's up?"

"Oh nothing. I saw you walk into the room, so I figured I would say hello. Can I put my stuff down in here? There's nowhere else to study." She sits down without waiting for me to answer.

"You can. But my girlfriend will be joining us soon. It's going to smell like Chinese food in here when she gets back with our food."

"Girlfriend? When did I approve of this?"

"Yeah. Her name's Michelle. I didn't know I needed your approval."

229

"So that's who I've seen you holding hands with in the halls."

"Stalk much?"

"I'm no stalker. I'm happy for you really. But she isn't what I expected for you."

"Neither did I. And that's a good thing, I suppose. I like to make my life decisions based on how surprising that are to you, Vanessa." I say without remorse.

"Don't tell me you're in love, Aaron. We were just fooling around in my apartment a few months ago."

"Not really something I want to define at the moment. And I'm not sure what you mean."

"We were in love once. Have you forgotten?"

"No, I haven't Vanessa. And I still have love for you. Did you need something? It doesn't look like you are trying to do much studying."

"Don't be so dramatic. I'll get out of your hair before your little girlfriend arrives. But I've been thinking. I think, I let you get away, Aaron."

"No, Vanessa. I moved on."

"I saw how badly you wanted me before. I should have let you have me then."

"That was then. Now has nothing to do with that."

"I don't want you to break up with your girlfriend, Aaron. I just want you one last time. It can be our little secret. I swear no one will know." Vanessa says while propping one of her legs across my lap.

I can feel how soft and toned her legs are. They remind me of how warm they kept my ears during those reckless escapades we called love. As intoxicating her presence makes me feel, my mind frantically pushes these urges at bay; I slide her leg off of mine.

"Vanessa…I say this not to hurt you, because I do care about your feelings. You and I at this time can't be more than just friends. Not while I am with her."

"It's just sex, Aaron. Michelle will never know. You were okay with this when you were with Helen. What's so different?"

"It's not that Michelle won't know. It's that *I* will know." I emphasize to Vanessa.

"So, would you tell her?"

"I would indirectly tell her. I've been there before. How could I look into her eyes the same way again? How can I truly say that our relationship is real while lying to her? I don't want to know where that road would lead. If we broke up, I would regret not giving this relationship my best foot forward. For right now, I want to focus on getting this right the first time." I end.

Vanessa isn't particular pleased with my response. She covers her legs up more with her jacket while collecting her things. "She's lucky to have you, Aaron," Vanessa says as she's about to leave. She gives me one last kiss on my cheek as she leaves the study room. I hug her good-bye without saying a word. I cradle her smaller frame against my shoulders and silently wish her the best. Vanessa deserves someone who is going to be faithful to her as I will be to Michelle. She's a great person and I know firsthand how awesome things can be with her. It's not her fault I wasn't ready the first time we met. It's not my fault, she was ready after I left. The timing never seemed to work with us. For a split second, I wonder if I am making a mistake when the room goes silent again. The thought dissipates when I smell the aroma of rice and honey. Michelle opens the door and livens the room up with her smile.

Chapter Thirty-Nine

Asking for More

Wednesday, Terri must have been bored. She always wants to know when I am in town, even though I never come see her. It's hard to maintain much of a friendship with your ex's best friend. But a part of me entertains her for the history we share since high school. She's still trying to find her way in the single world.

"Aaron, when are you going to be back in town."

"Thanksgiving. Next week." I reply.

"Nice. You got any plans?"

"I am bringing my girlfriend home. She's going to meet the family and friends."

"Does that include me?"

"As long as you remain *friendly*."

"Oh Aaron, you are old news. I have a man now." Terri texts me.

"Thank God."

"You don't have to be rude. We should still hang out."

"Will your man be there?"

"Depends…"

"…"

"No. But I would still like to meet your girlfriend. Is she nice?"

"She's wonderful. You would like her. I'm more nervous about if everyone else will like her. She's only the second person that I will have brought home to meet my parents."

"Wow. I can't wait to meet her."

"I still haven't made any official plans."

"Well, how about we get the gang together for a Friendsgiving before Thursday?"

"We'll see. I'll ask Michelle if she's up for it."

"Oh, never mind. I actually have plans on Wednesday with my new guy."

"I guess that settles that."

Terri always seems to be so nosey about what I am doing. She knows that I am not interested but she continues to keep tabs on me. She means well, but I seriously doubt that if I were to proposition her for a quickie; she would decline. I guess after Helen got married, she's had more time to finally get a man. Good for her.

Michelle is so nervous to meet my family. She's already been in my house, but it seems like it will be her first time. I reassure her that my family is typical and rather plain. The only novelty about us is the abundance of chop sticks and sandals at the door. She thinks I'm joking. We have a few more days to get ready before the weekend, so hopefully her nerves improve. I met her parents during fall break. They seemed to love everything about me. I tend to crack jokes when I am nervous to lighten the mood. They probably found it hilarious that I spoke fluent English. It is what it is.

Friday night while hanging out with Michelle at her place, Terri is calling me this time. I was sure it must be a mistake, because she never calls. I excuse myself to answer and leave Michelle to her chocolates during the movie.

"Aaron. I have to tell you something."

"Ok. I'm kind of busy at the moment. Can you call me later?"

"Is she there?"

"Who?" I whisper.

"Michelle. Michelle Miller?"

"Yes. How do you know her last name?"

"Facebook. Apparently, she and my last fling used to talk."

"Ok. Why are you telling me?"

"I take it, she hasn't told you."

"Tell me what?"

I distance myself further from Michelle to gather more privacy. I don't think Michelle cares that I am on the phone.

"Your new girlfriend is not so innocent."

"You don't even know her."

"I know people like her, Aaron. They seem perfect at first but their reputations catch up. You should be careful."

"I don't need your advice."

"If you don't believe me. You should ask her. How many guys has she slept with?"

"And what difference does it make to you?"

"You should ask yourself that—I could be so much better to you than her."

"So, you just assume if she and I don't work out, then you would be next on my list? I've heard enough. Bye."

I hang up the phone and am visibly upset. Michelle pauses the movie and checks on me.

"What's wrong, Aaron? Who was that?"

"Nobody. I don't even know why I answered."

"What did they say?"

"It was my ex's best friend. She told me that I should be careful. And that you were trouble."

"That bitch. Did she say anything else? Why is she calling you to tell you that? Give me the phone, let me call her."

"She said she was dating your old friend. I don't even know who that would be."

"Oh."

"Oh? Would she know you?"

"What did you say her name was?"

"Terri."

"Yeah. That is the name of the girl that my friend from Memphis is seeing. Well, I guess *was* seeing."

"It doesn't matter. It's a free country. And apparently a small world."

"Why are you so upset then?"

"She said that you were promiscuous and I deserved better."

Michelle walks away and starts crying in her room. I chase her but she's already locked the door. I can hear her sobbing. I try to squeeze in a question in between her breaths.

"Honey! What's wrong?"

"Aaron, I don't want to talk about it."

"Talk about what?"

"Any of this. You should leave. This may be all a bad mistake."

"Why are you crying?"

"I feel like this is always going to be a problem."

"What is that? Do you think I care about how many boyfriends you've had?"

"You would if you knew."

"Try me. I'll go first."

"…." She says nothing.

"Are you still there?" I ask.

"I'm waiting for you tell me, Aaron."

"Well, I'm not proud of it, but I've been with 5, maybe 6 different girls. No wait. It was seven. There was that one person who needed help in Algebra."

"Twenty." She says paired with a sigh.

"TWENTY?!"

"See Aaron, I knew you would get upset."

"No, no, no…. I'm sorry. I didn't mean to sound upset. I was just didn't know. I always thought you were the shy type."

"Guys are just an escape for me, Aaron. They were meaningless and most were only one-night stands."

"…" Now I'm speechless.

"Are you still there?" Michelle asks.

"Open the door silly. Let me talk to you."

She slowly opens the door and reveals her newly dried eyes.

"When I first met you, you were the first person that didn't find me as funny. Now we make each other laugh."

Michelle is smiling again as I reach for her chin.

"When I first kissed you, I felt like it was our last first kiss. It wasn't. But it felt like it."

She smacks my chest with a grin.

"When I first made love to you, I could hardly control myself."

"Oh, I remember."

"When we make love now, you make me forget all my troubles."

I kiss her and hold her closer.

"I don't care about yesterday. I don't need to know about your past, to know that I want to be a part of your future. Since we've been together, I've grown into my own. I've found who God meant for me to be. My past isn't picturesque either. But every blemish and regret made, shaped me to appreciate you better. I loved you before I ever met you. And I will continue to love you forever."

"I love you, too, Aaron."

Michelle removes her shirt and throws it at my face. Her perfect C-cups are exposed and she's pulling me towards her bed by my belt. I make sure that the door is locked behind me. I remove my shirt and pick her up by her thighs. I powerbomb her onto her mattress. She lets out a squeal of joy and amazement from my strength. I kiss her on her neck, making my way over to her earlobe. She begs me to slow down as her body flashes with excitement.

I do not relent. I remove her sweatpants and underwear simultaneously with force. She quickly places her palms to hide herself. I can tell she was caught off guard. I keep my pants on just to tease her further. Now she's becoming impatient. We trade positions many times during the night. Each time, she moans louder and louder. I can tell she has never been this satisfied before. We stop when we hear the next-door neighbors pounding on the wall, begging for us to keep it down. I ignore them because Michelle is asking for more.

Chapter Forty

Graduated

Graduation is here. Yes, time flew by that quickly. Michelle and I will be crossing the stage together. She will be waiting for me at the other end of the stage right before I get my diploma. Such a wonderful journey for each of us. Who would have known that college days swiftly pass? I look in the mirror and fix my tie once again, securing my cap tightly. Underneath the black gown, only my shirt and tie are revealed. I wear a bright golden tie to contrast my attire from the rest. Michelle has on heels and a blue dress underneath her gown. She even makes her billowing cape look amazing.

Our family is somewhere in the crowd waiting for the procession to start. Hearing the auditorium fill with the harmonics of the symphony band, brings tears to my fellow classmates. I've met most of these people sometime throughout the four years. The moment is a joyful one. Michelle is in front of me helping make sure my tie is on straight as well. She just wants to show me off. She gives me a kiss before the line starts to move.

On our way to our seats in the open crowd, I can hear the cheering roar throughout the air. Thousands of people are here to see us graduate. Families from all over the country

came to see us. I recognize a few random faces in the crowd.
The officer that pulled me over years ago is rooting for his
own daughter. Dr. Dallas is seated with the many professors
decorated in their doctoral colors. Nicole, Kurt, and Mark
also managed to make it. Jesse is already seated ahead with his
college of business peers. I can see the trail of sweat leading to
his seat. The anxiety of not tripping on my gown is racking
my nerves. I slowly calm myself by twiddling with my
graduation cap, firmly pressing it against my head. We finally
make it to our seats without any slips. I breathe a heavy sigh
of relief. Why couldn't Jesse be in the college graduate line
after mine?

Right before they begin to call our row up to the stage. I
reminisce on my current milestone. I think of my family, my
friends, and all the people that brought me to this moment.
On my mind, a beautiful round diamond solitaire, one point
five carats, H in color, internally flawless, worth all of my
earnings from the last three summers. I saw it in a storefront
over Christmas shopping last December. Michelle was
looking for a bracelet but I saw her eye catch on the refracting
ring's glimmering shine.

We are all asked to stand, and one by one we march to the
stage. On the stage are leaders of the University. I recognize
their faces and have memorized their names over the years.
They give each and every person a hug and a handshake as
they pass by. Michelle shakes the chancellor's hands and

receives her diploma. You can hear our families scream our names as we continue forward.

"Big head ass boy!" Mark screams at the top of his lungs.

The audience erupts in laughter but the mood continues to carry on our joys. After receiving my handshake, I close one chapter of my life. I race to catch up to the next.

Michelle is waiting for me at the bottom of the stairs at the end of the stage. My dad is ready with the camera and all of our family is there to directly tell us congratulations. Michelle turns to face them and wave whenever her father comes down with a bouquet of flowers. She's soaking in the moment. She doesn't realize that I've removed my cap to uncover the ring that I've hidden. Down on one knee, I tap her hip to regain her attention. She doesn't notice me there at first until I clear my throat with a cough. She gasps as she becomes aware of my intentions.

"Michelle Miller. I've known you since the very first day of class. You've been my best friend throughout all of these years. I fall deeper in love with you every moment that we share…"

"Aaron… is this for real?" She says after dropping the bouquet to cover her mouth in disbelief.

"…You are the one person that I want to spend the rest of my life loving. I appreciate how incredibly focused you've made

243

me. The way you laugh improves even the worst of my days. There is no such thing as a sour moment between us."

"Stop playing, Aaron! Get up from tying your shoe." Michelle is shaking her head. I open the box to reveal how serious that I am. Her jaw is agape and now the rest of the students begin to cheer. I manage to finish my proposal so that Michelle can hear.

"It would be my everlasting honor for you to be my wife. Michelle, will you marry me?"

"Yes! Of course, yes!" She exclaims without hesitation.

I retrieve the flowers from the floor and embrace her in my arms. I pick her up off the ground as she kisses me. She is crying tears of joy. She had no idea this was going to happen. People clap and applaud her acceptance of the ring. Students don't wait for the graduation to end. They begin to throw their caps in the air in celebration. The chancellor congratulates us, but informs the rest of the students to please postpone engagements until *after* the remainder of the graduation program.

We rendezvous outside and take a group photo together. Ellis is nearby and comes over to congratulate us on the engagement. He takes credit for hooking us up. My dad asks for us to group up and take a photo together. Michelle and I are in the center, while everyone else gathers around us to give us a big squeeze. I can't help but smile.

L. MAXWELL

Extra Chapter

Her Perspective

"Do you need help changing Vivian's diaper?"

"Nope. I got it honey." Aaron says to me.

    He is always so hard headed. I had a baby, I didn't lose my ability to walk. He's so cute when he tries though. Let me grab the wipes before he makes a mess.

"Honey!!! I need the wipes. Oh, how did you know?"

"You're welcome."

"How did I get so lucky? You're the perfect wife. Now I've learned you are the perfect mother to my child."

"Stop trying to get laid. The doctor said six weeks at the earliest remember."

"No, I'm serious honey. I wish we could've dated sooner. I don't know why I took so long to date you."

"Well it wasn't like I was waiting around with nothing to do. I had my own issues, remember?"

"I didn't know."

"That's because I never told you."

"Well, I'm yours now. Tell me. How did you end up becoming Mrs. Plattenburg?"

About the Author

L. Maxwell

Born in San Diego, CA, Maxwell later moved to Memphis, TN, where he spent the majority of his adolescence. He is the youngest with three older siblings. He holds a Bachelor's of Science in Chemistry and a Master's in Business Administration from the University of Tennessee.

Max got his love for writing during high school and college, but pursued the sciences professionally. He decided that writing will always be a major part of his passion and spent nearly two years to complete "Friends, Lovers or Nothing".

He spends most of his days solving the world's supply chain problems. In previous careers, he's been a scientist, technologist, banker, salesman, and currently a tech geek.

Max resides in Queen Creek, Arizona with his wife, daughter, parents, and dogs. When he isn't working or writing, you can find him playing basketball or playing his guitar. Max also enjoys tinkering with gadgets, cars, and electronics. Catch him online at https://www.facebook.com/LMaxwellWrites/

Made in the USA
Columbia, SC
09 March 2019